Flirting in Traffic

Beth Kery

ELLORA'S CAVE
Blush®
ELLORASCAVE.COM

An Ellora's Cave Publication

www.ellorascave.com

Flirting in Traffic

ISBN 9781419966958
ALL RIGHTS RESERVED.
Flirting in Traffic Copyright © 2009 Beth Kery
Edited by Ann Leveille.
Cover art by Dar Albert.

Electronic book publication March 2009
Trade paperback publication 2012

With the exception of quotes used in reviews, this book may not be reproduced or used in whole or in part by any means existing without written permission from the publisher, Ellora's Cave Publishing, Inc.® 1056 Home Avenue, Akron OH 44310-3502.

Warning: The unauthorized reproduction or distribution of this copyrighted work is illegal. Criminal copyright infringement, including infringement without monetary gain, is investigated by the FBI and is punishable by up to 5 years in federal prison and a fine of $250,000. (http://www.fbi.gov/ipr/)

This book is a work of fiction and any resemblance to persons, living or dead, or places, events or locales is purely coincidental. The characters are productions of the author's imagination and used fictitiously.

The publisher and author(s) acknowledge the trademark status and trademark ownership of all trademarks, service marks and word marks mentioned in this book.

-

The publisher does not have any control over and does not assume any responsibility for author or third-party Web sites or their content.

Chapter One

Esa laughed with a mixture of amusement and exasperation as her best friend poked at her shoulders and herded her out the door like she was a cow in the Chicago stockyards.

"What's with you?" Esa asked as she closed the office door and locked it.

"I've got a date at six," Carla said, her face glowing with excitement and the new foundation product she'd bought on the internet last week while she was *supposed* to be filing Esa's Medicare claims. Esa sighed. That's what she got for hiring her down-and-out best friend to be her administrative assistant.

"You're nuts. We'll never make it downtown by six in Friday night construction traffic."

"We don't have to make it downtown," Carla said with a self-satisfied expression. "We just have to make it to the viaduct on 63rd and the Dan Ryan."

"You have a date with someone at 63rd Street and the Dan Ryan," Esa repeated dryly.

"Well, not exactly. It's not so much a date as it is a checking-out-the-goods session. Kitten's reporter called it a Scheduled Traffic Flirtation, I think."

Esa's steps slowed as they crossed the parking lot. She'd caught a nose-full of trouble on the cool autumn breeze. It was hard to say whether it was the reference to her hugely successful, size four, mischievous little sister or the mention of her ridiculously popular magazine for single young Chicagoans, *Metro Sexy*, which had the more pungent odor.

"Scheduled Traffic Flirtation?" Esa asked warily.

Carla giggled hysterically as she grabbed Esa's arm and hurried her to the awaiting red convertible.

"You didn't read the article in *Metro Sexy*, did you? The one about singles flirting in Dan Ryan construction traffic? I'm the one who gave Kitten the idea," Carla squealed with irrepressible excitement. "I've been waiting for the right moment to tell you. I'll explain everything once we get on the road. Give me the keys, I'm driving."

Esa caught a quick glimpse of vanity plates that read *SXKITN69* on the back of her sister's racy Ferrari convertible. You'd think she'd been driving naked to work for two days given all the lewd stares, shouted indecent proposals, suggestive cell phone waving and creeps following them off the interstate. Esa'd practically killed them during Smoky-and-the-Bandit style evasive maneuvers, trying to lose the horny jerks while Carla laughed hysterically in the seat next to her.

Kitten—*Rachel* that is. Esa refused to call her sister by that stupid childhood nickname—lived and worked downtown. Otherwise there was no way in hell her extremely pretty little sister would put up with the ridiculous behavior Esa had been forced to endure while driving that racy sports car to the suburbs. But maybe Rachel just considered such idiocy part and parcel of her sexy image.

Suddenly her sister's insistence that she trade cars with her took on a sinister aspect. Rachel had claimed that she needed a more *staid* vehicle for her extended business trip to Indianapolis.

That was Esa all right, the staid, stodgy, boring, older Ormond sister.

"How long have you been planning this?" Esa asked as she got into the passenger seat. She realized that she sounded bitter but in truth she *was* a little hurt that Carla and Rachel had been plotting together without her knowledge. Sure, she was the gerontologist in the family and not the life of the party, sexy publisher but she was still a fun-loving city gal, wasn't she?

Or at least she used to be.

Carla, Rachel and she used to regularly stay out until three or four in the morning on the weekends, dining out at the trendiest restaurants, helping to plan Junior League charitable functions and then dressing to the nines for the lavish events, skipping out of work early on a Friday to catch a Cubs game, dancing and drinking at the clubs and creating all sorts of mischief in the romance arena.

The appeal of being a carefree Chicago socialite had dimmed quickly, however. Esa grew weary of the backbiting and vicious sniping between women. In addition, her parents—who used to wear patient, vaguely amused expressions when she and Rachel discussed Junior League events—could hardly be considered high-society headliner material.

"We haven't planned it for long," Carla said with a wave of her hand before she pulled on her seat belt. "A month or two. Long enough for me to have organized the Dan Ryan Construction Flirting chat loop online."

"The *what*?"

Carla's ecstatic expression faded quickly when she glanced down.

"Oh shit."

"What?" Esa asked, more confused by the second.

"I forgot it was a stick shift."

Carla's blue eyes looked enormous when she met Esa's gaze. Her lush lower lip, shiny with freshly applied lip gloss, poked forward in a pout. Esa knew from years of experience that Carla's "helpless blonde" expression reeled the sharks in like filet mignon on the end of a hook. Fortunately for Esa, she was both a straight female *and* a vegetarian.

"I can't drive a stick shift!"

"I know you can't. I was wondering what you thought you were doing," Esa replied with a smirk.

Carla's eyelids narrowed speculatively. The manic gleam returned. "You'll just have to drive." She plopped the keys into Esa's lap and clambered out of the driver's seat. "I told Vito I was a blonde bombshell. You're an auburn-haired girl-next-door. He'll never mistake you for me. What difference does it make who's driving?"

Vito? Esa mouthed in silent incredulity. Her knuckles turned white as she gripped the car keys. This just kept getting better and better, didn't it? She still hadn't moved when Carla flung open the passenger side door.

"Well?" she asked breathlessly. "Come on, Esa, you owe me after forcing me to go on that boring medical bookkeeping seminar last month."

"I sent you on that all-expense-paid seminar in Des Moines, Iowa because I *thought* you might want to improve your job skills," she muttered between tensed lips. Carla gave her a bland look.

"All right, I'll drive. Under one condition," Esa added when she saw Carla grin triumphantly. "Tell me everything about this stupid idea. I want to know precisely what kind of idiocy I'm going to have to bail you and Rachel out of."

"You won't be able to bail us out if you're in the clinker right there with us. Come on, Esa, picture it — a yummy, muscle-bound, bronzed construction worker-dude glazed from perspiration after some serious labor in bed." Carla's eyes sparkled merrily. "Don't *tell* me you're not thinking about how fun it would be."

Esa didn't put up too much of a fuss when Carla insisted she put down the top on the convertible once they'd reached 67th Street on the Ryan. The crisp fall air felt refreshing on her skin and temporarily made her forget that she was breathing the fumes of thousands of trucks and cars that communally moved like a gargantuan glass and metal slug on the pavement. Now that she understood that Carla's "date" wasn't actually mobile—some psycho stalker who could follow them into the city—but a stationary target, Esa felt a little better about her friend's crazy scheme.

"Since when have you been attracted to construction workers?" Esa asked as they inched forward in the clogged river of vehicles. The gargantuan project to widen I-94, otherwise known as the Dan Ryan, was already the stuff of urban legend even by Chicago standards, where everyone knew there were only two seasons—winter and road construction. The Dan Ryan project wasn't so much highway construction as it was road building on an epic scale, like the Romans used to do. Commuting from Esa's downtown loft to her suburban office had become a downright nightmare.

Carla waited for the rattling 'L' train next to them to pass before she answered. "Are you blind, Esa? You must be the only straight woman in Chicago who isn't drooling over those hunks while you're driving to work in the morning. I mean, there's got to be—what?—*thousands* of them parading around out there. The only thing better than tight butts in jeans are *flexing* tight butts in jeans." Carla checked her lipstick quickly in the mirror. "Steely thighs, bronzed biceps, broad shoulders—"

"Anything holding these guys' body parts together?" Esa asked, her voice dripping with sarcasm. "It's a good thing I drive us to work or you'd be helping other horny woman in the city contribute to Chicago's traffic nightmare."

"Just stop it right now, Esa."

Carla's sharp rebuke nearly caused Esa to plow into the Ford Taurus in front of them.

"What's wrong with you?" she asked Carla in dawning amazement. Carla hardly ever got truly pissy, which is exactly what she appeared to be at the moment.

"I should be asking you the same thing," Carla said as she hurled her lipstick into her makeup bag like a deadly missile. The scowl she wore marred her otherwise pretty, perfectly made-up face. "Or better yet, I should be asking you who you are and what you did with my best friend Esa Ormond. Clearly someone has stolen her and replaced her with some kind of alien robot whose idea of a good time is to write journal articles on the pros and cons of Viagra use and attend bingo night at the Shady Lawn Nursing Home."

"Carla, listen—"

"No, *you* listen. I tried not to complain too much when you started to refuse to go out with Kitten and me. I figured you'd just been burned a few too many times dating and were starting to focus more on yourself and your career."

"I did want to focus more on my career—"

"But *no*," Carla continued, oblivious to Esa's interruption or the loud beeping of the car horn behind them when Esa didn't immediately scoot forward ten feet in traffic. "Instead you gave up everything. You've forsaken *any* type of the usual fun that a twenty-nine-year-old single woman has. *Ever.* You won't so much as go out to have a drink with Kitten and me on a Friday night so we can laugh together or hang out with us to catch some rays on North Avenue Beach. Why don't you just go ahead and get your room reserved at Shady Lawn Nursing Home before your thirtieth birthday?"

Esa grimaced. As if she really wanted to put her near-nude, mile-wide curves on display next to Carla and Rachel's svelte, gym-hewn bodies at the beach. But she'd be damned if she'd give Carla the satisfaction of saying that out loud.

"I'm Shady Lawn's physician, Carla. I can't help it if I have to spend so much time there."

"You have more fun socializing with those old coots than you do me!"

The driver behind them gave up laying on the horn and glared at Esa as he passed in the next lane. Esa was too busy staring at Carla in stunned disbelief to even notice. Finally she clamped her mouth shut and shot forward a long stretch of road.

"Well, that certainly came out of nowhere," Esa muttered after a moment.

Carla sighed. "Sorry. But I'd be lying if I said any of it wasn't true. You're no fun anymore, Esa."

"I'm *fun*," Esa snarled.

"Sure, the residents of Shady Lawn think you're the life of the party," Carla muttered under her breath. She noticed Esa's glare. "Okay, if you're so fun, prove it. If Vito's all he's cracked up to be I'm meeting him and a few other chatters from the online traffic group for a drink at One Life, that new club on Huron Street downtown. Go with me? Please?"

Esa hesitated, thinking about all the medical charts she had stuffed into her briefcase. Carla's scolding warred with her practical nature. Even though she'd been acting so superior in regard to this whole flirting in traffic affair, Esa had to admit that it felt kind of good to have Carla beg her to take part in a loony scheme.

"I guess it'll be interesting if nothing else."

"Perfect." Carla clapped her hands happily before giving Esa a concerned look. "You're going to at least take off your glasses before going in One Life though, aren't you?"

Before Esa could unclench her teeth, Carla's blue eyes overtook half her face. "Look, we're almost to the 63rd Street viaduct."

"What's this Vito supposed to look like anyway?" Esa asked, curious despite herself. Her gaze flickered over the road construction to the left of the car, a vast landscape of cranes, drills, broken-up concrete, exposed rebar and hard-working men. The project was so massive that a full crew would work until nightfall. At that point gigantic lights would be illuminated and abbreviated work would continue until well past midnight.

The sight of a man exiting the door of a construction trailer snagged her roving gaze. Her eyes widened. Maybe Carla was right about this sexy-construction-worker thing.

Talk about a long, lean slice of pure heaven. This guy was some serious eye candy. Esa focused on the subtle rolling motion of trim hips encased in low-riding, clinging jeans as he came down the stairs, work boots stomping.

Those long legs and that sexy saunter would have caught her eye anytime, anywhere. Surely a guy who moved like that just *had* to move well in bed. At five-foot-eight-inches herself, Esa liked a tall man. She wanted to feel feminine in comparison to a date, not like Durgha, Queen of the Amazons. Maybe she was brainwashed by a sexist society but was it too much to ask for a man who she'd bet without a doubt could beat her in an arm wrestling match?

She found herself staring fixedly at the fullness behind the construction guy's fly. She blinked dazedly. A warm, tingling sensation flickered in her lower belly and simmered down to her sex. The sensation took her by surprise, it had been so long since she'd experienced it.

She glanced forward just in time to stop them from plowing into a Dodge Intrepid.

The man drew her gaze again like a magnet, however. Her eyelids narrowed in fascination as her gaze traveled up a whipcord-lean torso that slanted tantalizingly to shoulders that weren't necessarily brawny but extremely muscular and perfectly suited to his build. The dark blue t-shirt that he wore covered what Esa guessed were powerful biceps but left a pair of strong, tanned forearms exposed. He crossed them below his chest in a casual gesture when he paused next to a pickup truck that had just come to a neat stop next to him.

Esa was so busy mentally slobbering that it took a few seconds to realize that Carla was talking.

"I know what you're going to say. Guys can say they're Brad Pitt's twin online and then you meet them and they're more like Quasimodo's uglier brother but I don't know, Esa. I've got a feeling about this guy. He's six foot three, dark blond hair, works out regularly at his club in addition to all that hard work that he does during the day so you know his body's got to be rock-hard, thirty-one years old—"

A prickle of apprehension went through Esa when the man in the truck suddenly stopped talking to Mr. Adonis and looked point-blank at Esa. Although his face remained mostly in shadow, she saw his chin make a subtle pointing gesture. The man she'd been checking out so shamelessly turned around and pinpointed her with his gaze. Even at a distance of twenty feet that stare lasered straight through Esa.

"We're here. This is it. Go slow, Esa," Carla ordered in obvious excitement as they neared the 63rd Street viaduct. She sat forward in the passenger seat and examined the thirty or so men working in the vicinity.

"All right, all right," Esa muttered under her breath as she pressed on the brake. She suddenly felt self-conscious and silly, like she was in the seventh grade and at the roller rink passing a cute boy standing on the sidelines. A hysterical laugh tickled her throat at the thought.

She glanced over nervously at the two men, still feeling the one's stare like a light caress on her neck and shoulder. "I don't suppose Vito said he had blue eyes."

"Oh my God, Esa, that's *him*," Carla said under her breath when she finally zeroed in on the Adonis standing next to the truck. "Heaven help me, I'm in love."

Chapter Two
✺

Esa experienced a flash of jealousy at Carla's proclamation. *She'd* seen him first, after all. Her ridiculous proprietary attitude only grew when Carla gave a high wattage smile and waved. She glanced over in time to see Vito's hand go up slowly in a return greeting. He said something quietly to the man in the truck. Esa saw a flash of white teeth when he grinned at something his friend said. Carla giggled in the seat next to her.

Cocky bastard, Esa decided irritably. She threw him a sour look before she glanced ahead.

"Carla, what the hell am I supposed to do now?" Esa hissed. "It's clearing ahead of me. I can't sit here and block traffic while you flirt."

Carla ransacked her bag, never taking her eyes off Vito. She withdrew her cell phone and held it up for him to see. "It's okay, Esa. You can drive. I've seen more than enough," Carla conceded breathlessly.

"What are you doing?" Esa asked as she stomped on the accelerator, leaving Vito in her proverbial dust. That smirk on his face really bugged Esa for some reason.

"I gave Vito my cell phone number online. He's going to call if he…you know…likes me."

"Why does *he* get to be the one to decide?" Esa asked irritably. "What a conceited bast—"

But her tirade was cut off when Carla's cell phone started beeping the tune to a popular rap song.

Esa stewed while Carla giggled and simpered, catching phrases like, "Gosh, you must get so tired after working so hard in the sun for almost twelve hours...Oh you poor thing...Are you going to be at One Life then?...What?...I can't believe you lied about that. You are *so* bad...Seven-thirty? Sure, we'll be there..." And then as Carla ducked her head and faced the passenger door, "Yeah, I really liked you too."

Esa rolled her eyes as she changed lanes. So touching to be a witness to lust at first sight.

"How do you know he's not setting up dates with every woman on that stupid flirting chat loop, not to mention every single female advertising for a man in *Metro Sexy*?" Esa accused the second after Carla hung up.

"Esa, you're such a bore. We're not planning on marriage and two point five children. It's just for fun!"

"It's just for *sex*," Esa corrected.

Carla laughed. "And your point is? Sex *is* fun, Esa. It's not my fault you've forgotten that."

Esa simmered in the seconds that followed, unable to come up with a sufficiently acidic comeback. Besides...Carla was right. Wasn't she always encouraging her older adult patients to continue to express their sexuality in a safe manner? Sex was a crucial aspect of human behavior after all.

Lately, however, Esa preached much better than she practiced. At what point had she become such a prude?

The question rankled.

She mentally schemed for a way of getting out of going to One Life with Carla but for some strange reason Vito's grin kept popping behind her eyes like a cocky little dare.

She'd go all right...to protect Carla. Her friend was used to swimming with the sharks but Esa's intuition hinted that this particular animal was downright dangerous.

* * * * *

Esa peered at her reflection in the mirror. For some asinine reason she'd actually listened to Carla and gone to the lounge at One Life to remove her glasses. She really only wore them when she drove anyway, but all that talk about how boring she was certainly caused her to make a point of checking her appearance.

The sounds of a live reggae band filtered through the walls. Maybe it was the sensual beat of the music or maybe it was just all the reminders of how lame her life was that coaxed Esa to unfasten her blouse one button...then two.

She gave her reflection a shaky grin after she caught a glimpse of the shadowed valley between her breasts. Not sexy Kitten Ormond perhaps, but Esa still knew how to hold her own at a place like One Life.

The music immediately enveloped her once she left the ladies' room and went in search of Carla, whom she'd left sipping a sidecar and casting anxious glances toward the entrance. Her step faltered when she saw the back of a tall man wearing jeans, leaning over and talking to her friend. She scowled when she noticed the burnished brownish-blond hair and tight buns.

Well, apparently Vito had arrived and was getting right down to the business of making time with Carla. Or *Jess* had, anyway. That was one of the many things that Carla had gushed on about after she'd hung up her cell phone earlier. *Vito* was really a *Jess*. Obviously Jess was a tad more concerned about meeting clunkers online than Carla and was protecting his identity. Why the gorgeous Jess needed to use a chat group in a singles' magazine to land a date, Esa couldn't fathom.

Probably dumber than the concrete he poured on the job.

Her good friend's hoot of delighted laughter pierced through the music. Esa veered toward the bar, suddenly much in need of a stiff drink. Jess and Carla obviously weren't going to miss her.

After she'd finished half a martini, Esa felt lightheaded. When was the last time she'd actually had one of these, anyway? Esa wondered as the band broke into *Red, Red, Wine*.

Her body instinctively moved to the rhythm. She'd always loved the reggae classic.

Someone took her hand. Her mouth opened, the protest she'd been ready to utter melting like powdered sugar on her tongue when she looked up into the face of the man who held her fingers lightly.

Esa supposed the time period between when she stared into those arresting, amused blue eyes and when he spoke was only a few seconds but her brain stretched it surrealistically long. Her heart skipped erratically beneath her peek-a-boo cleavage when Mr. Adonis smiled—not cockily like she'd imagined from a distance. No, instead that slow grin was the equivalent of potent foreplay. Ever so briefly, his gaze flashed down to her chest...as if he were a magician and knew precisely what effect he was having on her.

"Would you like to dance?"

Esa nodded, thoughts of loyalty to her friend evaporated to vapor by the brilliance of his smile. Carla? Carla *who*?

He tugged teasingly on her hand and she followed him out onto the small dance floor in a mesmerized state. When he turned and released her hand they immediately began to dance to the earthy rhythm without saying a word.

Hadn't she guessed as she watched him come out of the construction trailer that the man knew how to move? He did all right.

Did he ever.

Esa's gaze drifted over a handsome face and an angled jaw slightly whiskered with dark blond stubble before lowering over a blue and white button-down shirt that set off his golden-hued tan. His collar-length hair was a blend of light brown, blond and platinum hues that mingled together in a tousled, sexy mess. He must have showered after work because he'd changed clothing and Esa could smell his soap and the subtle, spicy scent of his aftershave.

She looked down even further. The carnal rhythm of the music seemed to grant her permission.

Her hips moved with his in a tight, controlled roll to the sensual beat. A warm, tingly sensation of excitement swelled from her lower belly to her sex as her pelvis gyrated in perfect synchrony to his.

When Esa finally looked back up into his face again her breath caught in her throat. He no longer seemed slightly amused. Instead his face had gone rigid. His eyes had taken on an almost dangerous glint. Esa wondered what it would be like to have him pin her with that stare while his cock pinned her down to the bed. A muscle leapt in his tanned, lean cheek, and Esa had the strangest feeling that he was reading her mind.

Considering the fullness behind his fly when she'd been shamelessly staring just now as they rocked their hips in unison, it wasn't too much of a stretch to suppose he was thinking *exactly* that.

He spread one hand on her hip in a possessive gesture, bringing her into contact with his body. She bit her lip to prevent a moan of excitement when she pressed against him. He was erect…deliciously full.

Liquid heat flooded her. Her nipples tightened against her bra. Even the smooth, silky slide of her blouse seemed to abrade and excite the sensitized crests. She longed to press them against his chest to alleviate the ache and leaned forward to do so…

But the music ended.

"We gotta couple here who really knows how to *move* together," said a voice that was flavored with the accent of the islands. "If dey smoked on that one, they're gonna burn a hole in the floor wid dis one…"

The sound of the lead singer's voice broke through Esa's bespelled state. She blinked, realizing she was pressed tightly against a very attractive, aroused male animal.

A sexy, aroused male who was also a complete stranger, not to mention her best friend's date.

"Excuse me," Esa mumbled.

She staggered into the women's room. The reflection that peered back at her from the mirror only vaguely resembled the one that had been there on her previous visit. Her cheeks and lips were flushed. Her russet-colored eyes sparkled like she'd just swallowed a shot of potent liquor. Her wanton dancing had opened her neckline further and the ivory lace of her bra peeked out from the edge of the silk.

She looked thoroughly debauched.

Esa took a deep, unsteady inhalation and turned on the cold water tap. God, she'd *never* been flipped so effortlessly into the sexual "drive" position in her life. Just the thought of the hot look in Vito's—no, *Jess'*—eyes when she'd gyrated against his erection made heat flood her all over again.

She sighed dispiritedly and splashed some cool water onto her hot cheeks. Why did Carla end up with all the luck?

Esa gasped when she exited the women's room a half a minute later and found herself sandwiched between a hard, yummy-smelling man and the wall.

"Don't you know it's rude to entice a man like that and then just disappear?" he asked in a low, slightly raspy voice that caused goose bumps to rise along the back of her neck.

"Sorry," Esa whispered as she looked up at him. His smile told her that he'd been teasing. Light angled across the upper portion of his otherwise shadowed face, making his eyes seem to glow with heat as he examined her intently. Maybe he hadn't been kidding after all...

"I got sort of...hot, dancing," Esa muttered, not even sure what she was saying.

His mouth tilted further with humor. Esa watched, mesmerized, as that sexy smile descended. He growled softly before he covered her mouth with his.

He plucked with firm, persuasive lips once, then twice, seeming to assure himself that he had her agreement. It was Esa herself who opened and craned up for him, requiring no coaxing.

His taste inundated her with a tidal wave of lust. His agile tongue stroked lazily, explored her thoroughly. Within ten seconds they were kissing with a wild, hot abandon. The amount of suction he applied was perfect, creating explosions of sensation in her body that were far, far from her mouth, making it imperative that she rub up against him.

He was warm and hard...everywhere. When she fully registered the impressive outline of what strained behind his fly she moaned in mixed arousal and misery and broke his kiss. She grasped for a measure of sanity but it was difficult to think with his long body pressed against her and his male scent filling her nose. Her hands rose of their own accord and explored his muscular back with hungry fingertips.

"You taste so *good*," he murmured, sounding genuinely amazed. He nuzzled her ear and then lightly bit her earlobe, making Esa press her pelvis tighter to his, desperate to alleviate the ache that grew there with alarming speed. His hands cradled her waist and squeezed ever-so-slightly, as though he were taking her measure. When he gave a groan of satisfaction Esa was left with the definite impression that he liked the way she fit him.

She turned her head, blindly seeking out his mouth again. She moaned in excitement as she bathed once again in his intoxicating taste and their tongues dueled, teased and probed. *Sexual chemistry at its finest*, Esa thought dazedly.

"Let's get out of here," he mumbled against her hungry, nibbling lips a moment later. It gratified her to hear that he sounded as breathless as she was. "I don't live far away."

Esa's eyes widened in surprise at his bold proposal, not to mention the fact that she was actually considering it.

"Wh...what about Carla?" Esa asked, amazed at her sheer wantonness as she craned up to slide their mouths together and nip at his lower lip.

"What about me?"

She peered over Mr. Yummy's arm to see her friend standing in the corridor, her blue eyes wide with wonder. Esa straightened and pushed at her seducer's chest but he refused to move.

"Uh...I'm...you're... Jeez, Carla, I'm really sorry about this," Esa said breathlessly, the full impact of what she was doing hitting her like a ton of bricks had just landed on her chest.

"Why?" the man and Carla asked in unison.

"*Why?*"

"Yeah, *why*? It does my heart good to see you making out with a gorgeous hunk." Carla winked saucily at the man pressing her to the wall. "You two were practically doing it standing up out there on the dance floor. From the looks of things you better go somewhere a little more private or risk being thrown in jail."

A low, sexy laugh rumbled in the man's chest.

"You're not mad that I stole Jess from you?" Esa asked Carla incredulously.

"*Jess?*" She pointed at Mr. Yummy. "*He's* not Jess. Jess's over there." She shifted her finger behind her to the table where she'd been sitting. "*He's* Jess' big brother Finn." Carla's eyes twinkled with mirth. "Ain't I sweet? I brought a Madigan male for you too, Ms. Ormand."

Finn leaned down and brushed her cheek with his warm lips. He spoke so softly that Esa doubted Carla could hear him where she stood six feet away.

"'She had nothing to do with it. I was raring to come and meet you ever since I saw you in that red convertible and you threw me such a dirty look. Even your scowl turns me on. So what do you say, Kitten? My offer still stands. 'Course, if your place is closer than mine, I'm all for that."

Esa's brain whipped and whirled like an out of control carnival ride. Why had he called her *Kitten*? Then Rachel's license plates flashed in her mind's eye. Oh...so he thought *she* owned that racy car. He thought *she* was the type to eye construction workers like they were walking slabs of luscious male flesh just waiting to be consumed by a carnivorous female.

He assumed *she* was the type to spend a night of lusty, raw sex with a complete stranger.

Excitement burned in her lower belly as she met his steady stare. Wasn't that precisely the kind of thing she needed to break her out of her boring rut? Let him think she was a carefree, carnal sex kitten. Maybe she *was* the type to steam up the night with a complete stranger.

As long as the complete stranger was Finn Madigan, anyway.

Chapter Three

ଚର

Esa couldn't believe she was actually doing this. She was leaving a bar with a man she'd just met and she had every intention of spending a night of hot, sweaty, meaningless sex with him.

She paused in the lobby to put on her coat but Finn was instantly behind her to assist. Nice manners for a blue-collar worker, Esa thought as he released her shoulder-length auburn hair from the confines of her coat and spread it across her back, his fingers delving through the length appreciatively before he let go.

"Your hair is beautiful."

Esa glanced over her shoulder and stared. Finn Madigan was really one breathtaking sample of manhood. She'd never seen eyes so blue in her life. Her mouth strained upward, seemingly of its own will.

"Thank you," she whispered.

"You're welcome," he muttered before he seized her lips again. They couldn't seem to get enough of the taste and sensation of each other. Esa had never experienced anything remotely like it in her life—as if she chugged pure, distilled craving.

And she realized something else. She'd never been kissed before tonight. Not like this. Finn made kissing the main event of sex instead of foreplay. He fisted her hair, bringing her closer and consuming her in hot, tempting ravishment. His other hand spread across her stomach and pushed her bottom against the fly of his jeans. He moved her against him with a tight, circular movement.

The bouncer sitting fifteen feet away wolf-whistled.

Esa broke the kiss and stared up at her tall, lean, thoroughly edible would-be lover with bemusement.

"We'd better get going." He grabbed her hand. The forbidding frown he threw at the bouncer as they passed instantly dampened the man's expression of lascivious amusement.

"Where's your car?" Esa asked as she hurried to keep up with his long-legged pace. If she had to guess she'd say that Finn was as anxious to do the horizontal tango with her as she was with him.

"I have a truck."

Why did he give her that sharp, knowing look when he said that, Esa wondered, like he suspected she was thinking—oh, of course *a truck*, big dumb construction worker that he was. Which she hadn't been thinking at all, or at least not the part about him being dumb. Something about Finn's incising gaze called to mind the polar opposite of stupidity.

"But I gave my keys to Jess. He lives in Bucktown and we can walk to my place," he added.

She glanced around in surprise. They were in the midst of Streeterville, just a block off Michigan Avenue, one of the most expensive, sought-after places for real estate in the city.

"You live around here?"

"A few blocks up. You familiar with the area?" he asked as he dragged her across a traffic-laden street.

"Sure, I've lived in Chicago my whole life."

"Me too," he said with quick grin. Esa stared, wondering if she shared ten thousand one-night stands with him the potency of his smile would fade. Maybe it had to do with the fact that the expression of his face was usually quite serious...intense. The appearance of his white smile was like the unexpected drawing of a blade, piercing straight through a woman's typical defenses.

"I grew up on the South Side."

"South Side Irish?" Esa asked.

"You got it. There probably isn't a stereotype in existence about a Chicago Irish South Sider that the Madigans don't completely embody."

"Lots of brothers and sisters?" Esa queried as she walked rapidly to keep up with him. She found his undisguised haste to resume their sexual exploration of each other to be sort of endearing.

"Yep. Seven of us."

"Die-hard Sox fans, one and all?"

"Is there any other baseball team in Chicago?"

Esa laughed, knowing quite well what her south suburban male patients thought of the Cubs. "And do all of your brothers besides Jess work in construction as well?

Once again there was that gleaming sidelong glance. Esa's grin wavered slightly.

"I'm the oldest. Two of my brothers are still in college. But Jess works construction and one of my sisters does too," he replied casually enough despite a censorial glance as he swung open a glass door for her. "Mary Kate was always one to thumb her nose at stereotypes."

Esa glanced around the luxurious lobby. Talk about thumbing your nose at stereotypes. She felt like everything was moving so fast with Finn...and in such unexpected directions. Unlike the lobby of her modern, Near West Side loft this place screamed of old, established money.

"Good for Mary Kate," was all Esa had the opportunity to say before Finn grabbed her hand again and pulled her across the lobby. The doorman greeted him warmly by name. A sedate buzz accompanied the opening of the security door. The elevator slid open immediately when it was called. Finn hit the button for the twenty-third floor.

The next thing Esa knew he was pushing her back against the wall of the elevator.

"You're not changing your mind, are you?" he asked softly just inches from her parted lips.

"No, of course not," she answered, recalling that Finn expected her to be a wanton who didn't blink twice at the idea of bedding a man she'd just met. The type who didn't fuss about the fact that they were being surveilled by a security camera while they were in a clinch in the elevator either, Esa assumed.

He dropped a slow, sultry kiss on her upturned lips and Esa forgot what the words "security camera" even meant. He raised his head to study her after a breathless few seconds.

"Good, 'cuz I'm gonna make you purr, Kitten."

He sank his blond head again for a kiss that made Esa's toes curl in her boots. His hand cupped her jaw possessively on both sides as he penetrated her mouth again and again. He kissed her as though he believed without a doubt that she would submit to every single one of his desires.

And Esa had to admit, Finn had the rare ability to make her believe it too…to make her *want* it desperately.

That must have been why she didn't protest when he removed one hand from her jaw and slid it boldly beneath her coat and blouse while he continued to kiss her silly. He filled his palm with her breast, shaping and massaging her before he flicked his forefinger against a nipple that strained against tight nylon. His hand was large, his fingers long. Esa felt strangely satisfied that her breast overflowed it.

She moaned into his marauding mouth when he gently pinched the stiff bud. He heard the plaintive sound and lifted his head. Esa stared up at him helplessly as he teased and flicked and agitated her hypersensitive flesh. She bit her lower lip to keep from crying out in acute pleasure when he angled his long body, sliding and pressing his cock into the juncture of her thighs.

His nostrils flared.

The sound of the elevator dinging open was highly unwelcome to both of their ears.

The cool air of the hallway did little to relieve her overheated state as Esa raced down it, Finn in the lead, already digging in his front jean pocket for his keys. He paused in front of a mahogany door, grimacing as he inadvertently tightened denim that already strained against his erection. He caught Esa's amused look and they exchanged a grin before he finally extracted his keys and pulled her through the opened door.

Something about that moment of shared amusement sent Esa over the edge and straight into the abyss of mindless lust. Instead of allowing him to lead her into his bedroom, she stole a page from his book and pushed him against the wall of the foyer. She was all over him immediately, her fingertips, lips and tongue starved for all that lean muscle and smooth, golden-brown skin.

Finn looked a little surprised when she plowed into him but he recovered quickly enough, returning her ardent kiss with hot passion and unsurpassable skill. Esa thought she'd never tasted anything as good as his mouth but she regretfully gave it up to sample his neck. She wasn't disappointed. He chuckled when she nipped at him playfully.

He cupped her bottom with both hands, bent his knees and brought her flush against him. This time when she nipped him he swatted her fanny lightly.

"Naughty kitten," he admonished.

Esa's already simmering body flashed up to the boiling point.

"*Bed*," he ordered.

Esa ignored his monosyllabic command. She was pleased to note that he didn't move, holding her to him tighter as she unbuttoned his shirt. She felt his eyes on her as she used her lips and tongue to sample the crinkly light brown hair and the smooth, warm skin that she revealed as she went.

Her tongue darted over a flat, copper-colored nipple. He beaded tight for her. He muttered something indecipherable and one hand rose to the back of her head. His fingers furrowed through her hair as she teased and agitated his nipple with her lips, tongue and nibbling front teeth. She subjected the other to an equal torment before she continued her downward journey.

Esa acknowledged that she'd never been this aroused in her life as she kissed his flat abdomen and the ridged, clearly defined muscles rippled with excitement. Her tongue dipped into his taut bellybutton. He was such a beautiful, sinuous male animal that it made her ache deep inside with longing. She knew that only he could alleviate that primal pain.

"Ahhh," he groaned when she tenderly cradled the fullness behind his fly in her palm. Esa knelt before him, her heart running madly in her chest. She'd never done anything remotely like this the first time she was with a man. She reached for the first button on his jeans. His fingers flexed in her hair in a gesture that seemed to both restrain and entreat her at once.

"Don't… I'm so turned on I don't know if I'll be able to…"

Esa glanced up at him and their eyes met. His facial muscles were rigid with restrained excitement. She liked that. She liked it a lot.

"I don't care if you stop or not, Finn. I want you."

She lowered his jeans and a pair of boxer briefs that looked starkly white against his tanned skin. She held his gaze as her hand slid along the long, smooth pillar of his jutting cock. His eyes blazed hot as he watched her with a narrow focus.

She leaned forward and delicately tested the tip with her tongue to see if he was as smooth as he looked. He was, but he was hard as steel beneath. She closed her eyes in sublime pleasure and slid him into her mouth.

Time seemed to stand still. She heard his guttural groan as if from a distance. Her entire awareness narrowed to the experience of his texture and taste. She couldn't get enough of either. She learned his most sensitive spots as well as the rate and pressure he preferred by the movement of his fingers in her hair.

Just before he made her stop, he gripped at her with a wild desperation that Esa loved. He restrained the increasingly avid bobbing motions of her head, however, and sank down on his knees next to her.

"Think you're real cute, don't you?" he asked, a hard glint in his blue eyes. He ripped open the belt of her trench coat.

It suddenly struck Esa that she was grinning like an idiot.

"Not cute, just extremely horny," she corrected shamelessly. The sudden appearance of his smile made her clench her thighs together to alleviate the pinch of lust there.

"I'm glad to hear it because I'm afraid this is going to be quick and dirty and you've got no one but yourself to blame."

She yelped and giggled when he pushed her backward and they fell into a graceless heap on the lush foyer carpet. He spread his hands on the outside of her thighs and lifted her skirt. She raised her hips, assisting him as he drew her panties down. A singular feeling of feminine pride surged into her breast when he knelt between her knees and stared down at her wantonly spread legs adorned only with pale thigh highs and her tight burgundy leather boots.

She hadn't considered herself as sexy very much lately but at that instant, when Finn Madigan went preternaturally still between her thighs, Esa *knew* she was.

"I must have done something very, *very* good today to deserve you." He met her gaze, his stare just as warm as his words before he rifled his jean pocket with barely restrained haste. Esa thought she would combust with excitement as she watched him slide a condom down his firm, proud erection.

Then the lovely weight of six foot and several inches of long, hard, very aroused man was back on top of her. He gave her a quick, scorching kiss as he positioned himself. Esa groaned at the sensation of the head of his cock nudging her moist entry.

He lifted his head and watched her as he steadily impaled her. Esa gasped when he fully sheathed himself in her body.

He looked a little crazed.

"God, you're perfect," he muttered as he drew out of her.

Esa gripped his buttocks and brought him back deep with a crisp whap of striking flesh, telling him without words that he was pretty damn perfect himself. Her actions seemed to light a fuse in him.

They began to mate wildly...frantically.

Esa was only vaguely aware that he took her with such force that her body inched slightly back on the lush carpet with each downstroke. But she matched his hard-driving rhythm eagerly. Her desire had built to an almost unbearable pitch even before he had fused his flesh to hers. It didn't take long for his demanding thrusts to pitch her right into the hot oblivion of an explosive climax.

When she blinked her eyes open a moment later he'd momentarily stilled. He watched her face with a tight, hard focus. He began to move again, at first slowly. But when she began to join him in their taut, fluid rhythm, he increased his pace until he surpassed even his previous one.

She scooted back on the smooth lining of her trench coat and yelped in helpless abandon as he struck their flesh together again and again. The friction built and swelled unbearably until Esa strained yet again for release.

He pushed her arms over her head. Her back arched, her breasts thrust upward. By fixing her wrists to the floor firmly he kept her immobile as he rode her hard to the finish line. She cried out when he lowered his head and sucked an aching nipple straight through her blouse and bra.

"Oh *God*," Esa exclaimed as climax reared over her yet again.

He groaned and pressed deep.

The feeling of his penis throbbing inside her as he came triggered her own shattering release. She shuddered as wave after wave of orgasm crashed through her.

A heart-pounding, hard-breathing moment later Finn nuzzled her breast. Esa sighed with contentment but already her body quickened around his embedded flesh.

He lifted his head and regarded her with a heavy-lidded look of amusement when he felt the intimate caress.

"Uh uh. You're not getting your way this time, Kitten. This time we go to the bedroom and do it right."

* * * * *

Esa touched the soft, steel-blue duvet cover on Finn's handsome king-sized bed with a sense of growing awe. The headboard was covered by a beautiful cerulean blue fabric — one of the few bold colors in an otherwise muted palette. The décor in this room was much like that of the rest of the condo that she'd glimpsed ever so briefly as Finn led her back to his bedroom before he went to the bathroom to wash up — tasteful, unique, luxurious yet austere.

All the furniture possessed simple, clean lines in colors of gray, blue and tan with an occasional accent of stark white. Floor-to-ceiling windows in both the living room and bedroom faced east, granting what must be a breathtaking view of Lake Michigan during the daytime. She realized that the colors used to decorate the entire condominium reflected the changeable moods of the lake and sky. Esa wasn't an expert on decorating but she didn't need to be to appreciate the overall effect of harmony and peacefulness that pervaded the silent condominium.

Or at least Esa wished that the surroundings of Finn's luxurious condo would calm her at present. Even the sounds of Finn washing up in the bathroom were muted by the thick pile carpeting. She shifted uneasily as she stared at an original contemporary painting mounted above the bed. Her gaze transferred to several oversized volumes on the coffee table in the seating area, with titles on architecture, art and design.

Nervousness flickered into her awareness for the first time that evening.

What did she really know about Finn Madigan? Since when did construction workers live in expensive, luxurious, tasteful Streeterville condominiums with prime lake views?

Since when did Dr. Esa Ormand have sex with a complete stranger on the floor of his foyer?

Suddenly the whole situation since she'd danced with Finn at One Life seemed surreal. She knew *nothing* about the man she'd just made shameless, passionate love to.

Panic flared in her chest, momentarily stealing her breath. God, at least he'd worn a condom. She'd have that thought to soothe her in her future sessions of self-mortification and mental cursing in regard to her promiscuous behavior tonight.

Esa tightened the belt of her trench coat with shaking hands. The water faucet shut off in the bathroom. Her eyes went wide in panic.

She bolted for the bedroom door like she thoroughly believed lightning was about to strike Finn Madigan's bed.

Chapter Four

Finn didn't speak when Jess walked into the trailer at eleven-fifteen the following morning, but he guessed he didn't have to by the sheepish look on his younger brother's face.

"Sorry I'm late."

Finn scowled and let the blueprints on his drafting table roll closed. He wasn't in the mood for Jess' excuses. Not this morning he wasn't.

As the second-oldest Madigan, Jess would have been the obvious choice for shouldering at least part of the burden for the welfare of the Madigan family. Mary Kate was the next oldest but she worked hard as a foreman for Madigan Construction and had three rambunctious children under the age of nine to consider as well.

The previous owners of Madigan Construction, Uncle Joe and their father Ed, had died within three months of each other this past summer. It had been a brutal double blow for the Madigan clan, one that had indelibly changed the trajectory of Finn's life. Finn's mother knew woefully little about the details of running Madigan Construction, even less about its financial workings and building contracts.

Molly Madigan had always been a busy housewife. Her husband, extended family and seven children kept her more than busy at home. Any spare time she possessed was spent volunteering at her church and in the community.

The shocking, unexpected death of her husband of thirty-four years had hit her the hardest of all, of course. Finn had taken one look at his mother's bewildered, shattered expression as he went through his father's office the evening after the funeral, trying to make sense of Ed's haphazard bookkeeping system, and known that his life was about to change forever.

That same night he'd made the decision to sell his shares in the architecture and engineering firm he'd established with his good friend and partner Jason Prevast. The firm had only been up and running for a few years and hard-won, lucrative contracts had just started to come pouring in. Jason had given him more than a fair price for his shares but Finn was no fool. He knew he'd walked away from not only an enormously fulfilling career but a financially rewarding one as well.

But if he didn't do something to whip his father's business into shape, Madigan Construction was not only going to end up floundering, but taking down the Madigan family with it into the murky depths of bankruptcy and monetary hardship.

He'd hated that he had to at least temporarily give up on his dreams. But life was a bitch sometimes, right? No reason to moan about it. He still had two younger sisters in high school, two brothers in college, his mother and his elderly grandmother to think about supporting.

He'd tried his best to plan for the painful, drastic alteration in his life. But fate wasn't satisfied until it threw him another unexpected blow. His live-in fiancée Julia, the woman with whom he'd believed he would spend the rest of his life, had been dead set against his decision to sell his firm and run the family construction business.

When she'd packed her bags and left just one month ago, Finn knew that she'd made her final decision. He'd made his own by letting her go without a fight. Julia was breathtakingly gorgeous, clever and confident but she wasn't the woman Finn had thought she was. Not by a mile.

Brains and beauty only went so far when it came to the nasty bumps on the road of life.

He figured it was best that he'd discovered before he'd married Julia, not after, that not only his financial status but his image as a successful, white-collar entrepreneur had been crucial aspects that Julia loved about him.

Finn had still been in the midst of a post-breakup funk when he'd seen Julia's face in the society section of the *Chicago Tribune* last week. She'd been on the arm of Galen Graves Jr., scion of a wealthy family from Wilmette and Chief Operating Officer for corporate giant Glen-Cat. Julia had worn that small, mysterious smile as she looked into the camera's eye, the one that used to drive Finn crazy with lust.

Why hadn't he ever noticed before how contrived that expression was? It irked him to realize he'd *never* know what had been genuine about her and what had been a lie.

The caption below the photo indicated that Julia and Gavin were the hottest new item on the social circuit. Even though Finn figured he was better off without Julia in his life, his bitterness had only grown when he saw that photo. Not so much toward Julia, but at himself for being so stupid as to be hoodwinked by her.

And never mind how much his anger had escalated when she'd cornered him in the lobby of his condo just four nights ago, eager to resume where they'd left off—at least in the bedroom anyway. Apparently it would have suited Julia just fine to have her picture snapped at high-profile charity events on the arm of Galen Jr. while spending stolen hours with Finn smoking up the sheets. But her brawny, blue-collar, would-be secret lover wasn't quite as biddable as Julia would have preferred, Finn thought grimly.

Yeah, a hell of a lot could change in a few months' time.

His brother Jess, however, appeared not to have altered his life plans in the slightest. Despite the fact that he held a prestigious degree in the biological sciences from the University of Illinois and probably had a viable claim to the title of "Most Intelligent" in a family of extremely bright people, Jess continued to pick up his Madigan Construction paycheck like an hourly employee. He still drank and socialized at Dooley's tavern almost every night as if there was no tomorrow and bedded any pretty woman who looked his way—which apparently was just about every damn one that he encountered, from the action Jess saw in a typical week.

His little brother still brimmed over with the mischief of a twelve-year-old at Catholic school, always looking for fresh opportunities for fun and excitement. Unfortunately he'd managed to drag Finn himself into his most recent misadventure involving that singles' magazine and an online traffic flirtation loop. Or maybe that wasn't fair.

Finn had been all too willing to plunge into trouble since he'd first laid eyes on the redhead driving the sports car. When Jess had suggested that he go to One Life with him earlier that evening and explained the circumstances, Finn had just shaken his head and rolled his eyes.

Then he'd seen Kitten and had an abrupt change of heart. She wasn't his type, of course. Finn didn't like the flashy look-at-me type who would drive a racy car with vanity plates. Kitten Ormond made him look, all right—he'd hardly been able to unglue his eyes from that bouncy, lustrous auburn hair or the disdainful expression in her brandy-colored eyes, glittering through her preppy glasses.

Maybe it had just been that his sex life seemed to have gone into dormancy ever since the traumatic death of his father and Julia leaving him. Perhaps it was just his body's way of telling him that it was time to get back on the often treacherous obstacle course of dating once again.

All Finn knew for certain was the redhead in the Ferrari made him randy as a goat.

It felt so fantastic to have lust pounding through his veins once again that he'd allowed himself to get entangled in one of Jess' stupid schemes. He had no one but himself to blame for the fact that he'd spent a sleepless night in an empty bed—a bed where he'd hoped to be making love to a curvy, responsive, fiery red-haired beauty.

But when he'd come out of his bathroom after washing up, raring to go another round...he saw that his cute, cuddly stray had bolted.

Finn had been stunned by her abandonment. Then he'd been pissed. His pride had been pricked by her abrupt departure. He wasn't a ladies' man on the par of his brother Jess but he'd had his fair share of women. And never once had one of them turned tail and run while he was in the midst of making love to her.

"I guess from that sour look on your face you didn't get lucky last night like I did," Jess said smugly, pulling Finn out of his reverie. "I'm surprised. That little redhead was smoking. Great body—plenty of flesh and all in the right places. And what a rack—" Jess paused abruptly in the action of holding his hands over his chest in a cradling gesture when Finn frowned at him forbiddingly.

"So what'd you do to turn her off? I hope you didn't go on about Julia. Women are wary of guys on the rebound. My guess is that you sent her running by lecturing her about the necessity for haste because of the freezing temperatures of asphalt and concrete?"

"No, I save that lecture for you. Not that you ever listen."

Jess glanced up in surprise from where he was dumping powdered creamer both into his mug and onto the metal table. "Hey, are you really that pissed about me being a few hours late? Nobody else has to work on Saturday. What good is there in being the boss if I can't enjoy an armful of warm, sexy woman in my bed on a weekend morning?"

"If you don't know by now I doubt you ever will."

Jess touched his fingers to his eyelids in a characteristic gesture of martyrdom—the one that signaled he was about to be bullied by his sanctimonious big brother. "Christ, Finn. No other contractor on the Dan Ryan project is as riled up about making deadlines and keeping costs to a minimum as you are.

I mean, *come on*. If we don't finish it we'll just make up for it in the spring. It's only government money."

"Yeah, Jess. State and federal money. Money from taxpayers like Mom and Grandma Glory and you and me."

Jess gave him a droll expression and swigged his coffee. Finn should've known better than to use that argument. It never worked on his brother, who seemed to have extremely blurry vision when it came to focusing on matters of ethics and moral conscience.

"All right, look, if that doesn't set a fire in your belly consider this. The state was always Dad's and Uncle Jo's best employer. They got contracts from them year after year because they worked their asses off to bring in almost all their projects on time."

"Lot of good it did them," Jess said glumly as he plopped down at a desk that was covered with foot-high stacks of paper. "Let's face it, Madigan Construction is hardly Fortune 500 material."

"Madigan Construction gave you the financial means for a secure, happy childhood, private schools, a college education. Thanks to its growth in the last year, it'll do the same for the next generation—"

"I *know*, I know." Jess put up his hands to stave off Finn's familiar lecture. "Christ, sometimes I think Dad skipped rebirth and just reincarnated straight into you. You sound exactly like him sometimes."

"Thanks."

Jess started and met his brother's gaze. He hadn't meant it as a compliment, of course, but he saw Finn's point. They'd all worshipped their bigger-than-life, quick to smile, charismatic father. There wasn't one Madigan who wasn't still sore from the wound of his abrupt death.

"You're welcome," Jess conceded under his breath as he stood and set down his mug. "So, what's on the agenda, fearless leader?"

"I need you surveying at that new stretch we contracted two weeks ago. We need to make that a priority before—"

"Snow flies," Jess finished the familiar litany with a roll of his eyes.

"It's true. We'll have an extra month or so with the viaduct, since we're not as reliant on ground temperature."

"Jess?" Finn asked abruptly when his brother reached for the trailer door, surveying equipment cradled in one arm. Jess paused, his head ducked beneath the threshold.

"Your date last night... Did she say much about Kitten?"

"Who's Kitten?"

"The little redhead," Finn elaborated irritably, using language Jess would comprehend. When his brother still looked perplexed, Finn cradled his hands over his chest, mimicking Jess's former crude breast-cradling gesture. Comprehension dawned on Jess' face.

"Oh...right, the vanity plates. *Kitten*, huh? She was a hot one. I always was partial to redheads. Funny, I thought Carla called her something else. Carla and I didn't have much opportunity for talking about buddies, if you know what I mean." He flashed his patented Don Juan smile. Molly Madigan's gamine green eyes took on a whole new definition in her second-oldest son's face. "Why? What do you want to know about her?"

What did Finn want to know? He wanted to know plenty. How many men Kitten Ormond had entertained between her thighs in the last month, for starters. Why it was that even though he wouldn't like the probable answer to that question, he still couldn't stop thinking about the vibrancy of her laughter, the excitement of discovering the depths of her sensuality...the look of vague surprise intermingled with intense pleasure on her lovely face when she came.

Or why the hell she'd made love to him like a sizzling firecracker on his foyer floor—exploding several times to amazing effect—only to leave him high and hard in a cold, empty bed?

What did Finn want to know about Kitten? Her goddamned phone number would be great for starters.

Despite his self-admonishments for doing it, he'd already tried to call her using directory assistance this morning. Kitten Ormond's number was unlisted.

Maybe one of the most crucial things he'd like to know was why he cared about all those things one way or another. Kitten probably thought he was nothing but a blue-collar stiff without a working neural pathway in his brain, a slab of male flesh who conveniently didn't require batteries.

Finn knew the type.

If he'd been forced to admit it, he also knew why he'd tried to contact her this morning. The sex had been phenomenal. Incredible. Electric. He'd had a take it or leave it attitude toward sex since Julia left him.

But after Kitten, he was in the mood to take it all right. In spades. He wasn't looking for any serious commitment, granted. Not after everything he'd just been through. Fortunately Kitten seemed like the type who was just out for a good time, which worked just dandy for him.

He was certain she'd enjoyed the sex as much as he had so he'd sure as hell like to know what made her run out of his condo like she was a fugitive. Surely he owed her at least a phone call. What if something catastrophic had occurred?

"I want to know how to get in contact with her but she's not listed. Could you ask Carla for her number?"

Jess shrugged before he headed out the door. "Why don't you make things easier on yourself and just call Caleb? It's not like you don't know the little minx's license plates," Jess said with a lascivious rise of his eyebrows. He stuck his face back in the crack of the trailer door before he shut it.

"And hey...if you manage to find her try not to let her get away this time, okay? This is exactly what you need—a hot fling to help jolt you out of this depression you've been in since Dad died...and since Julia left you."

Finn just gave his brother a bland look. In truth, he was none too pleased that he'd resorted to his little brother's tactics for soothing grief, not to mention a bruised ego and a boatload of self-doubt. The image of Esa scowling at him from the driver's seat of that Ferrari flashed across his mind's eye.

Rebound reaction or not, Finn was going to find her.

Finn glanced at the marquee in the lobby of the modern, sleek high-rise on Michigan Avenue. He sensed the security guard's forbidding stare on him. Shit. He probably should have changed out of his dusty work clothes before coming. He'd rather catch Kitten off-guard by knocking on her front door instead of scaring her off with a doorman's phone call. But the security guard was never going to allow him on the elevators to the exclusive residential section of the building without an okay from Kitten.

He studied the marquee while secretly scamming how to get past the guard. A mane of dark red hair caught his attention out of the corner of his eye.

He nodded once at the security guard a few moments later as he headed toward the bay of elevators on the left—the ones that led to the businesses instead of the residences. He stayed at a distance and watched while Kitten got onto an elevator by herself.

The floor indicator showed that she got off on the twenty-first floor. He pushed the up button.

What a stroke of luck. Not only to have seen her, but that she'd gone to the business section of the building instead of the residences. His cousin, Illinois State Trooper Caleb Madigan, had been the one to inform him of Kitten's address. Caleb had whistled into the phone when he'd traced the license plates.

"Pretty fancy digs, Finn. Thought you weren't interested in the high-flying type after Julia."

"Just give me the address, Caleb."

"And this wipes my debts clean from the last poker game?" Caleb had asked anxiously.

"Yeah. You're free until I take all your money again at Grandma Glory's Halloween party."

That had been sufficient assurance for his cousin. "All right, but you didn't hear any of this from me."

Within seconds Finn had had one Kitten Susan Ormand's vital statistics at his fingertips, including her home address and telephone numbers.

Finn was familiar with the building where she lived since his firm had been located just blocks away on Pearson Street. He and Jason occasionally came here for lunch at an Italian restaurant on the third floor.

He stepped off of the elevator. There were only three large offices on the twenty-first floor—an insurance business, a real estate company and the offices of *Metro Sexy* magazine. The latter was the only one that showed any signs of life.

Metro Sexy—wasn't that the name of that singles' magazine that had organized the asinine flirting in traffic scheme that Jess was involved in? Jess...and apparently Kitten as well. Kitten's bold license plates flashed into his mind's eye. Could it be that Kitten worked as well as lived in this building?

The door was unlocked. Although the receptionist's desk was empty, the person who manned it must have just stepped away for a moment, given the evidence of an opened bag of chips and soda can sitting next to the keyboard of a powered-up computer and the radio tuned to a local station.

Otherwise not a sign of life stirred in the luxurious offices.

Finn headed toward the walnut-paneled hallway behind the reception area. He hesitated only briefly when he saw the sign that read *Kitten Ormand, Publisher* next to a partially opened door.

She sat behind her desk. The sight of her caused a surprisingly strong feeling of grim satisfaction and possessiveness to surge through him. Her expression of stunned disbelief segued to one of rising panic when Finn shut the door behind him with a brisk bang and narrowed the distance between them.

"We have some unfinished business, Kitten," he informed her.

Chapter Five

Esa conveniently transferred her anger at herself for sleeping with a complete stranger onto her sister. *Rachel* was the one who had set the stage for her impulsive, completely out of character behavior with all that insistence that Esa drive her glamorous fast car and plotting with Carla about that stupid flirting in traffic chat loop. She'd been *planning* for Esa to get some action.

As if Esa wasn't capable of getting a man in bed on her own.

If she wanted to, anyway. Which she hadn't. Not until Rachel and Carla foisted Finn Madigan on her.

What sane woman would refuse *him*?

Her fury had only escalated when Rachel wouldn't answer her cell phone. Esa knew perfectly well that Rachel's phone had practically been grafted onto her ear since she was twenty years old. So her refusal to pick it up the morning after Esa's ignominious night of sexual promiscuity was undoubtedly intentional. Obviously Carla had gotten to Rachel first and spilled the news about Esa leaving the bar with the drop-dead gorgeous Finn.

She and Rachel were very close but there were times when Esa was sorely tempted to wrap her hands around her sister's swanlike throat and give a healthy squeeze.

Esa reached a sleepy-sounding Carla as she drove down Lake Shore Drive to visit her parents in Evanston. She didn't even give her friend a chance to say anything but a groggy "hello" before she launched into her attack.

"Tell Rachel to stop avoiding me."

"Well, good morning to you too. What are you so grouchy about?"

"I'm not grouchy. Just tell Rachel to stop avoiding me. Is she on your other line this second?"

Esa could tell by Carla's prolonged pause that she'd guessed accurately.

"You already told her about Finn, didn't you?" Esa snarled even more than she'd intended when a silver Porsche cut her off. What was it about driving a sports car that brought out the competitive idiot in everyone? She jerked Rachel's convertible into the outside lane and sped past the Porsche.

"Why, is there something juicy to tell?" Carla asked brightly.

"Nothing whatsoever."

"Uh-huh," Carla replied skeptically. "I hope you're not p.o.'d at me for not correcting Finn when he called you Kitten last night before he asked you to dance. He got the idea from the license plates. I just thought it was sorta funny considering how you hate Rachel's nickname."

Esa's eyelids narrowed in the bright sunlight bouncing off Lake Michigan. Finn had made *a lot* of mistaken assumptions about her thanks to Rachel's sophomoric vanity plates. "Why does everyone insist on calling Rachel that stupid name? She's twenty-seven years old for God's sake, not a gum-smacking Mouseketeer."

"It's sexy—fits her image. She's had it legally changed, you know," Carla stated matter-of-factly.

Esa rolled her eyes. She wasn't in the mood to talk about Rachel's sexy image. "Carla, listen to me. Listen very carefully. I forbid—do you hear me?—*forbid* you to say a word about me to Jess or Finn Madigan. Pretend like we hardly know each other."

"Why?" Carla asked, clearly shocked. "Don't tell me you're trying to avoid Finn. Esa, he's the most delectable, yummy—"

"He's a *man*, Carla, not a midnight snack."

Esa almost groaned out loud when she registered her own words. Apparently she'd been of a different mind last night when she'd kissed and licked Finn's beautiful bronzed torso before she'd dropped to her knees and—

Heat flooded her cheeks.

"He's the best kind of snack," Carla continued suggestively. "The decadent kind that makes you *burn* calories instead of pack on the pounds. So what are you in a tizzy about? Obviously Finn wasn't as entertaining as his little brother. I say *little* only in regard to their ages, mind you, because Jess is far from being little in *any* other sense of the word."

"Thanks for that completely unsolicited piece of information," Esa grated out. "Now, two things—one, tell Rachel I'm going to catch up with her so she better stop avoiding me. And two, if you say a word to Jess Madigan about who I am or what I do for a living, you can start looking for a new job come Monday."

"Jeez, don't hold back, Esa. You'll get an ulcer if you keep in all that acid instead of spewing it out all over your friends. Do *I* even get to ask you how things went with Finn?"

Esa shot a dirty look at a blonde woman who shot past her in a dark blue Lamborghini. She punched the accelerator and zoomed past her challenger. Driving a fast car did strange things to people's personality, no doubt about it.

"How did things go with Finn? They went awful. *Terrible*. Now you know, so the answer to your question is *no*. Don't ask me any more about Finn Madigan. Not if you value our friendship."

Esa understood why her parents hadn't answered the phone earlier this morning when she found that their handsome, lovingly restored Victorian home was empty except for Felix and Sylvester, their two fat cats. She eventually discovered her mom and dad on their hands and knees in their beloved garden.

"Morning, sweetie." Lexie Ormond waved a handful of dried-out cattail stalks in the air. She grinned when Esa dropped a kiss on her proffered cheek and straightened her floppy straw hat in the process. "Having dinner at Marisa Cartland's tonight. Don't want to be sunburned. She's thinking about selling her house—too large now that her kids are in college."

"Think she'll let you sell it?" Esa asked, referring to her mother's profession as a residential real estate agent.

"You know your mother. She'll have the listing by the time hors d'oeuvres are served," her father said. Esa smiled when she saw that he'd just smeared some black soil on his nose as he adjusted his glasses. David Ormond was a professor of physics at Loyola University. His perpetual vague, distracted expression and rumpled clothing coincided with his brilliant yet spacey academic persona perfectly.

He grinned sheepishly when Esa wiped the dirt off his nose.

"Gorgeous weather for October. Kitten said it was ten degrees cooler in Indianapolis," he said.

"Rachel called this morning?" Now she possessed solid proof that her sister was avoiding her!

Esa's anger had simmered just below the boiling point the entire time she helped her father plant a maple sapling in the backyard. It didn't diminish when, despite her mother's protests, Esa manically raked all the fallen leaves in the large backyard into a great pile.

"The neighborhood kids will have them scattered all over the place by evening," Lexie said thoughtfully as she inspected her daughter's efforts.

"Give the little monsters hell if they even *look* like they're going to jump in my leaves."

"Oh, Esa, lighten up. Where's your sense of fun?" Lexie murmured with a little laugh before she set off for the house.

Esa ground her back teeth. Was her own mother in on the *clobber Esa with the message that she's a grouchy bore* plot as well?

She turned down one of her mother's delicious lunches, saying she had some important errands she needed to run. She didn't tell her mellow, easygoing parents that her crucial errand involved finding a way to chew out their flighty youngest daughter.

Esa broke a few land speed records driving downtown to Rachel's office. She planned to coax Rachel's administrative assistant into giving Esa the name of her sister's hotel. But she'd forgotten that it was Saturday and had instead found only a skeleton staff at the offices of *Metro Sexy*. The receptionist recognized her as Rachel's sister, however, and allowed her to go to Rachel's office in order to leave a note. Esa would probably speak to Rachel before she got it, but in the meantime it gave Esa an outlet for her fury.

Esa had been in the midst of penning her nasty, scathing missive when seemingly out of nowhere Finn Madigan walked into Rachel's office.

Her first reaction to seeing his unmistakable form just feet away from her was amazement that she was experiencing a hallucination. But surely hallucinations weren't so clear. No, the hard angles of his face, the eyes that were currently narrowed on her into concentrated pinpoints of vivid blue light, the sheer vibrancy that seemed to roll off his long, lean body in waves...one couldn't imagine anything that breathtaking.

What could he be doing *here*?

Then he'd called her Kitten and Esa felt like howling in irritation. Of course the frivolous, promiscuous sex kitten that he supposed her to be was worth going to any length for a virile male to locate.

"What...why are *you* here?" Esa croaked through a dry throat as Finn Madigan ate up the space between them.

"I told you. We have some unfinished business."

Esa swallowed heavily but it couldn't abate the rapid leaping of the pulse at her throat. "I-I—"

"You walked out on me," he finished succinctly. He was so big that the top of Rachel's desk only reached him at mid-thigh. Esa found herself staring up at a tall tower of glowering man.

"I-I can explain about that," Esa said in a rush.

He crossed his arms. "Okay. I'm listening."

Esa glanced down in blind desperation at the note she'd been leaving Rachel and frowned. In her anger she'd not only inadvertently called Rachel her childhood name of Kitten, she'd also spelled *interfering* wrong. She hastily turned over the note and stood. She couldn't think straight with Finn Madigan staring down at her from such a superior height.

"I realized that I had to be somewhere else," she said. She picked up a marble paperweight on Rachel's desk and began fiddling with it nervously.

"And you don't think you could have let me know that before you left without saying a word?"

"It just came to me all of a sudden while I was..." She trailed off.

"While you were sitting on my bed waiting for me so that we could do it right?"

The paperweight landed with a loud thud on Rachel's desk. Her gaze shot up to meet Finn's. How could his voice have sounded soft and suggestive when his eyes burned through her like surgical lasers? He'd taken her so off guard that she said the first thing that came to mind.

"You got it *right* the first time."

"That's what I thought. So how come you scrammed?"

Esa's backbone straightened when she registered his grin. Finn was clearly just as cocky as she'd guessed that first time she'd salivated over him while he strutted around the side of the highway like the king rooster in a hen house.

"I told you," she said with a chilly tone as she rearranged Rachel's paperweight, hoping the large crack that nearly cleaved it in half had been there before. "I had to be someplace else. I'm not quite sure why I owe you an explanation anyway. How did you find me here?"

"Where?"

"Where? *Here*," Esa explained with a trace of exasperation as she glanced around Rachel's office.

"No, I mean where did you have to be in such a hellfire hurry last night?"

She glared at him. He screamed of insouciant incredulity as he stood there with his arms crossed, his hip slightly cocked and a smirk on his handsome face that stated loud and clear that even though he was asking, he wouldn't believe a word she was about to say. He had a lot of nerve, treating her like she was a second grader who kept insisting that her homework was devoured by the hungry bear that occasionally took up residence beneath her bed.

"I remembered I had a date," she told him with affected indifference as she picked up her purse from where she'd left it on the floor.

"'S 'at a fact?" Esa wasn't quite sure why, but for a split second she was sure that Finn had growled the question.

"Yes. It just slipped my mind until that moment."

"I hope you made it on time."

"Just the teeniest bit late," she replied sweetly. She came around the desk, trying to hide her trepidation at the idea of no longer having such a reassuringly solid object between her and Finn.

"So you had a good time on your date?" he inquired warmly.

"Hmmm?" Esa asked, losing the thread of their inane conversation when he suddenly turned and matched her pace as she fled the room. Her heart hammered so hard in her ears she almost couldn't hear her own voice.

From the corner of her eye she saw how crisply white his t-shirt looked against his tanned skin and the gray flannel shirt that he wore casually over it. If the pair of faded jeans that he wore fit his lean hips, long thighs and tight butt any better he'd have jean companies shouting out offers for him to advertise their product while he sauntered down the city street.

Yeah, Carla had pretty much been dead-on in her assessment. Finn Madigan *was* downright delicious.

The fact that he, like his brother Jess, was undoubtedly used to having sexy young things throw themselves at him on a regular basis didn't surprise Esa a bit. What infuriated her was that he clearly thought *she* was one of those vacuous, disposable creatures. He was only pissed off because she'd punched a leak in his swollen male ego. She'd dared to walk out of the line while most females were taking numbers and patiently waiting to get on the Finn Madigan ride. Most of them probably guessed correctly that he gave one hell of thrill while the ride lasted.

The thought pricked at her pride and made her draw up short just feet from the door.

"You know," she began with a condescending smile. "I had a really great time last night. But I wouldn't want you to get the wrong impression. I'm not interested in anything permanent."

"You drive a red sports car with license plates that read *SXKITN69*. Apparently you're the publisher of a magazine that my brother has decided is the holy bible for hooking him up with women that are as single-minded in their expectations as he is. You had sex with me on my foyer floor after dancing with me once at a bar. Why the hell would I think you were interesting in anything *permanent*?" he deadpanned.

Esa closed her slack jaw with a click of her back teeth.

"Of course you aren't," she said after a moment. "It's just... Well, why did you show up here then?"

He leaned down until she felt his warm breath ghost her forehead. His scent—a mixture of fresh air, the spicy remnants of his aftershave and the well-recalled singular smell of his skin—pervaded her awareness. Her nostrils flared as though to capture more of his essence greedily.

"I told you," he said gently but firmly, as though he was indeed dealing with a recalcitrant five-year-old. "We have business."

"You want to...to...hook up *again*?" Esa asked, embarrassment heating her cheeks at using that particular phrase in reference to herself.

He frowned. "What...you stick religiously to the definition of 'one-night stands', is that it?"

"Of course not, I just—"

"Look, the last thing I'm looking for is anything serious either so stop acting so jumpy. But the fact of the matter remains. I wasn't finished with you last night."

Esa met his stare, stunned by his quiet intensity.

Why had she fabricated that particular lie about not wanting anything permanent in a relationship? He already thought it of her, but it made her sound so unappealingly mercenary to have actually *said* it. And she suddenly wished— very, very much—that Finn Madigan would have gone to so much trouble in order to locate regular, boring Esa Ormond instead of the silly fantasy she'd created for him.

Now that she'd lied though, she felt foolish for taking it back. Especially since he'd indicated he was just out for a no-strings-attached good time.

Her gaze dropped to the hard line of his well-shaped mouth seemingly of its own accord. Still, there were so many benefits to the fantasy. The imposter woman had been allowed to kiss Finn's lips, to taste his smooth, golden skin...to burn beneath his long, lean body.

"What are you thinking?" he rasped.

Esa jumped. Had he just moved closer to her? The mouth that she'd just been fantasizing about was now only inches away from her own. She licked her lower lip nervously and froze when she watched his vivid blue eyes trace the movement.

"I-I was wondering if you thought one more night would do the trick?" she croaked.

Finn blinked and met her stare. His slow smile made heat unfurl in her lower belly. "If you promise to stay put and let me have my way with you all night...it just might."

Esa swallowed convulsively.

"So, do you ever allow one of your lovers to actually take you to dinner?" he asked.

Esa started out of her Finn-induced trance at that. Did he really think she was *that* promiscuous? A bitter defense rose to her tongue but she stilled it when she saw how his eyes glowed with arousal as he stared down at her mouth. Obviously Finn *wanted* her to be a loose, unprincipled sort of woman, so what right did she have to deprive him of his fantasy?

Never mind the fact that it was beyond thrilling to have him look at her like he was about to eat her up in one bite.

"Occasionally. A girl's got to keep up her energy," she informed Finn as she watched him through lowered eyelids. She wasn't sure if he bought her seductive act or was just laughing at her when his white teeth flashed in his tanned face. Her heart seemed to pause in her chest when he ducked his head and used those sexy teeth to nip at her lower lip, gently prying her open.

When his attack came, however, it was anything but subtle.

He cut off her shaky moan by covering her mouth, penetrating her lips with his sleek tongue and kissing her hard and thoroughly. The lights that flashed behind her eyes looked like colorful blooming flowers. When he released her from that total onslaught on her senses her eyelids remained closed.

"Who taught you how to kiss, anyway?" she mumbled.

He took his time answering her question as he tucked a wayward strand of hair behind her ear. "Let's see…that probably would have been my cousin Dina."

She opened one eye. "Kissing cousins? Isn't that a bit of a cliché?"

His low, rumbling laughter made her want to press her cheek to his chest and absorb the experience with another sense organ besides her appreciative ears.

"She's only a cousin by marriage, but then again just about everyone in Bridgeport is and the ones who aren't are the real thing," Finn said, referring to the South Side neighborhood where he grew up. He grabbed her hand. "Come on. How about a picnic? It's a nice day. We might as well enjoy it while we get you fueled up for action."

Esa opened up her mouth to protest his crudity—sex kitten act be damned—but then she noticed the gleam of mischief in his blue eyes. Her already escalated heartbeat skipped into double time as he pulled her out of Rachel's office.

Dangerous. The alarming sort, warning-was-not-sufficient, run shrieking for the hills and hide all the valuables—most especially your heart—kind of downright dangerous.

That's what Finn Madigan was.

Chapter Six

She had to admit, Finn knew how to do a picnic right. They'd stopped at a French restaurant on Walton Street where the man standing behind the empty bar greeted Finn by name. When Finn explained what they planned the middle-aged gentlemen—who appeared to have a genuine French accent—bustled about preparing their outdoor feast. He'd made eye contact with Esa when he drew down a bottle of Bordeaux from the wine rack, and winked.

"He really likes you, doesn't he? You must come here a lot?" Esa had whispered to Finn.

He'd shrugged. "I used to come several times a week."

"Don't you anymore?"

Finn had shaken his head. "Nah. I used to work across the street. Now that I'm at 63rd and the Dan Ryan it's a little far to drive for lunch, even for Paul's food."

Esa had opened her mouth to ask him more about his previous job but Paul called out at that moment, holding up a partial round of cheese. Finn nodded his approval and Paul added it to the paper sack already filled with a crusty loaf of bread, a package filled with marinated olives, a bottle of wine, a plastic wine opener, cups, napkins and two enormous fresh peaches.

After parking Rachel's car in the parking garage at Finn's condo, they'd strolled lazily down Lake Shore Drive to Millennium Park. Since the day was so beautiful and the park was fully decked out in brilliant autumn regalia, they'd walked a bit before settling down to eat lunch.

They'd paused to watch a group being supervised in park-sponsored pumpkin carving. One particular pair of participants had caught Esa's eye—a five- or six-year-old chestnut brown-haired girl accompanied by what appeared to be her grandmother. The older lady had successfully traced the pattern for the jack-o-lantern onto the pumpkin but she was wincing in discomfort as she tried to use a razor-type knife to carve out the meticulous design.

"No, it's too sharp for you, Melissa," Esa heard the grandmother tell the girl gently when the child tried to take the knife from her.

"Do you mind?" Esa asked with a friendly smile at the gray-haired lady as she nodded toward the hand that held the cutting tool.

The older lady looked confused by Esa's request but she held up her hand nevertheless. Esa took the woman's thin hand and removed the knife. Her fingers expertly massaged and soothed the arthritis pain that was clearly plaguing the elderly lady's hand while she tried to enjoy a golden afternoon with her granddaughter.

The woman was grinning broadly by the time Esa released her hand a moment later. "Thank you!" She flexed her fingers and her smile widened. "It feels so much better. You have a gift there, young lady."

Esa returned the woman's smile. "It was my pleasure. You two ladies have a wonderful day."

* * * * *

Kitten avoided his puzzled stare and headed quickly down the path away from the pumpkin carvers.

"What was that all about?" Finn asked when he reached her side.

"What? Oh, *that*? I'm good at massage. I get a lot of practice, you know," she explained with a sultry look. His return appraisal was frankly suspicious.

"Is that your way of telling me that your bedmates are usually in their seventies and suffering from arthritis?"

"You'd hardly fit the bill if that were true, lover," she teased.

The red-blooded male in him couldn't resist the heat in her brandy-colored eyes. He spread his hand on her lower back just above her right butt cheek. When he applied a slight pressure Kitten slowed and came to a halt.

He leaned down and planted a slow, hot kiss on her lush lips. *Christ,* she tasted good. When he realized that he'd turned her in his arms so that he could reexperience firsthand how well she fit against him, and that his cock had stiffened to full readiness with record-breaking speed, Finn regretfully broke their embrace.

When he lightly urged a dazed-looking Kitten to keep walking, he had to take several deep breaths to regain his equilibrium. He'd have to watch himself. Her taste did strange things to his body chemistry. He was supposed to be having a little fun with a sexy woman to get over Julia and pull him out of the dumps he'd been in since his father's death. At the rate he was going he was going to become thoroughly addicted to Kitten's sweet mouth—not to mention the rest of her succulently curvy body.

Whoa, he definitely needed to apply some brakes here. He reluctantly removed his hand from the enticing swell of her upper ass and grasped her hand instead. The dreamy, goofy look on her pretty face as she stared blankly into the distance reeled him back in to her sexy snare quicker than he could blink. Made him feel like a king that his kiss made her look that way—

"It looks like the sails of a ship unfurling," she murmured dreamily as they walked and she stared at the stainless steel curves of the Pritzker Pavilion, the enormous outdoor band shell that was the centerpiece of Millennium Park.

"That's a good description, actually," Finn said as he glanced at the pavilion, glad to focus his attention elsewhere than on Kitten's big, sexy eyes and lust-flushed pink cheeks. "A ship's beauty is a consequence of its function. Frank Gehry, the architect, might have pushed the aesthetics a bit to get the effect for the Pritzker Pavilion but everything on that band shell serves a purpose. See that?" he asked as he nodded at the intricate trellis of stainless steel pipe that domed the open air seats and lawn.

"It's the lighting system, isn't it?"

"There are lights on it, yes, but the entire structure is primarily a very sophisticated sound system. Gehry designed it to distribute and enhance the sound from the stage across the huge area of this lawn. The audience gets amazing sound from the stage but the entire structure, including the bridge over there," he nodded at the stainless steel bridge that serpentined across Columbus Drive, "was also designed to keep urban sounds *out* of the park."

"Awesome," Esa muttered as she studied the modern structure. Her speculative glance transferred to Finn. "How come you know so much about it?"

"How does a guy who breaks up concrete at the side of the road know anything about world-class architecture and engineering, you mean?"

"*No*," Esa retorted, clearly stung by the sarcasm he hadn't successfully kept out of his tone. "I didn't mean it like that at all. I guessed from some of the stuff I saw in your condo that you knew about architecture and design and stuff. I was just wondering where you learned it."

"Building viaducts and roads might not be pavilions and bridges but they're all in the same ballpark." He glanced once more, longingly, at the ultra-sleek structure. "We can't all have the high-profile gigs," he added in a flat tone that didn't invite further inquiry.

He was glad that Kitten didn't pursue the matter when he briskly suggested that they go eat their lunch.

* * * * *

The Crown Fountain had quickly become a favorite Chicago landmark, demonstrating interactive art at its finest. Esa chuckled as she watched dozens of children playing in the water that covered the enormous black granite courtyard between the two fifty-foot-tall fountain towers made of tiles of glass. The kids wore everything from swimsuits to rolled-up jeans and t-shirts, their shoes and socks long forgotten next to parents who lolled on the sidelines in the autumn sunshine, secretly envious of their children's opportunity to cool off in the water.

Their picnic was delicious, especially spiced as it was with Finn's warm, amused glances as she consumed it with relish.

"It must be at least eighty degrees. I was thinking about..." Finn stilled when Esa reached out and spontaneously wiped a stream of peach juice from his chin. Her eyes snapped up to meet his gaze when she realized what she'd done.

"Giving the fountain a try myself, I'm getting so warm," he finished huskily.

"Sorry," Esa said as she removed her fingertip from his skin. She took another sip of wine to calm her nerves.

For the most part, she found Finn to be an easygoing, fun companion. He had a rich supply of entertaining stories, which usually involved some colorful character from his large extended family winding up in some improbable and inevitably hilarious situation. Esa realized that she'd just spent almost two hours with him, however, and wasn't that much closer to knowing about Finn the man, except that he obviously loved his family like nuts.

It only made him exponentially more attractive to her. Not that he needed the extra help in that arena.

"There's nothing to apologize for. I grant you free rights to touch me anytime you like." He grabbed the hand that had just been stroking him, pressed his thumb into the center of her palm so that her fingers uncurled and bent his golden head to plant a warm kiss where his thumb had just been.

Esa shivered despite the heat that flooded her.

"Is that right?" she asked with forced casualness as she firmly extricated her hand from his grasp and leaned back in the grass. She reached into the paper sack and grabbed her peach in order to busy her hands while he studied her through narrowed eyelids. Despite her ease with Finn, her intense sexual attraction to him made her wary. Her body had never responded so wholeheartedly to any of her serious boyfriends in the past. It confused her to the point of feeling downright threatened that a weekend fling evoked such a reaction from her.

Although Esa had never been a very accomplished tease, she found it surprisingly easy to flirt with Finn. Every time she began to do so quite naturally, however, an alarm started blaring in her brain, warning her that she was behaving precisely in the shallow, promiscuous manner that he expected of her. Resentment would inevitably follow.

Why did men always have to be so predictable in the type of woman they wanted?

"Yeah, that's right," Finn replied. His handsome mouth twisted into a frown before he took another bite out of his peach, unashamedly letting the juice run down his chin again for a few seconds before he used his napkin to wipe it off. "I've never known a woman who runs as hot and cold as you, Kitten."

"I don't know what you mean," Esa replied airily as she watched the children splash and frolic in the fountain.

"Yes you do. You're giving me 'come and get me looks' one second and throwing poison darts at me with your next glance. Do you want to be here with me or not?"

Esa's lips fell open at his forceful question. "Yes," she replied honestly before she had the chance to censor her answer.

Flirting in Traffic

"Good." Finn paused before he resumed chewing a mouthful of peach slowly. "I apologize for that...earlier."

Esa's mouth fell open in amazement. "What are you talking about?"

"When I got so defensive about my job." He set the juicy peach on top of a paper sack and wiped his hands on the grass with an impatient gesture. "My fiancée just recently left me because I decided to sell my shares in the engineering firm I'd started downtown and run the family construction business after my father died. I guess I'm still a little sore about it. Didn't mean to take it out on you."

Esa swallowed and set down her own peach. Something about the flat, emotionless quality of his voice made her want to reach out and touch him, comfort him. Jeez, he was fresh out of a breakup from a serious relationship with a woman who sounded like a real loser. How could she have left him during such a difficult time in his life?

And this all explained why he wasn't interested in anything but a fun, no-strings-attached fling. Finn undoubtedly was looking for an escape from the recent-breakup-blues. Esa herself had engaged in a few similar, short-lasted euphoric affairs in her past. Sex could be a terrific balm to a scarred heart and wounded self-esteem, especially *great* sex.

Even though the realization that Finn was definitely unavailable in any emotional sense made Esa feel a little sad, she caught his eye and gave him a reassuring smile. "It's okay. You don't owe me any apologies."

He grinned. "My mother would disagree. She drilled it in to me to apologize for my occasional rudeness." He suddenly stood. "Come on, take off your shoes and let's go for a wade in the water. My hands are all sticky. I want to rinse them off."

Esa was doubtful about his order but she was grinning hugely by the time she walked into the shallow water of the fountain. "It didn't think it would be so cold," she told Finn between irrepressible giggles as she stood in the midst of dozens of capering children.

He paused in the action of rolling up the pant legs of his jeans and just stared at her for a second. Before she could guess what he was thinking he walked into the water with a determined expression on his face. He turned her around so that her back was pressed into his chest and forced her toward one of the two transparent fifty foot tower-fountains. Behind the glass bricks an enormous video screen scrolled through thousands of Chicagoan faces. Every five minutes or so one of the faces would purse its lips and a thick fountain of water would shoot from its mouth at the same time that sheets of water would flood down the towers.

Which, given the evidence of the shouting, jumping children that surrounded Finn and her, was about to happen at any second.

"*No*, Finn, it's about to—"

The fountain gushed with water, sheets of it pounding off the glass sides of the tower and splashing onto Esa's face.

Splashing onto Esa's *everywhere*.

"Oh!" she wailed as she clenched her eyes closed and water soaked her. When the fountain stopped cascading torrents a few moments later she opened her mouth to shriek a reprimand at Finn, but he stopped her by pressing his mouth to her ear.

"Sorry. I go a little nuts when I hear you laugh."

Her eyes went wide at that sweet, sexy comment being whispered in her ear. She inhaled his scent. She forced herself to ignore the effect that he always had on her but she wasn't very successful.

"I-I'm soaking wet," she moaned. As miserable as she knew she *should* be by her predicament, she still couldn't seem to focus on it with Finn's long, hard body pressed against her backside.

"I know," he said softly as he opened one large hand over her abdomen and pressed her back into his length. Even though Esa was drenched in cold water, heat flooded her cheeks. She clenched her thighs together tightly against a growing ache between them when he encircled her ribs, cradling the undersides of her breasts on his forearm.

"You don't know anything," she pouted halfheartedly. "You used me to block you from the water. You're almost completely dry. That's not fair."

"You want to play fair?" he asked as he transferred his mouth to her neck. Esa leaned her head over to give him better access. He moved his forearm ever-so-subtly, stroking the tender, sensitive skin of her lower breasts. Her nipples pulled tight inside her bra. She turned her head, instinctively seeking out his warm, supple lips, wanting...no, *craving* them against her own.

"Yes," she managed to say when he began to place warm, beguiling kisses on her lips. "But I want you to play fair too."

"Fine," Finn whispered. His blue eyes gleamed as he watched her and deliberately bit her lower lip with his white front teeth. Esa groaned and squirmed against him but he held her firmly. "Then come back with me to my condo so I can finish what you never let me start last night. We'll both feel relieved afterward. Don't you think?"

"Yes," Esa admitted before they came together in a quick, scorching kiss.

That's exactly what she needed — relief from this raging fever that Finn had ignited in her body. She felt as if she'd never had much of a choice in the matter. What Finn did to her was like encountering a force of nature. Better just to let the fire blaze until it fizzled out of its own accord.

"Kitten...how come you taste so damn good?" he mumbled gruffly when he released her mouth a moment later.

"Uh, Finn?" she asked dazedly as she looked up at him.

"Umm hmm," he murmured, his gaze still glued on her lips in a manner that made it difficult for Esa to concentrate. But this was too important to let pass.

"My-my real name is Esa. Kitten is—a professional name."

He stared at her for a long moment, making her wonder if his piercing blue eyes were dredging the depths of her lying soul.

"Esa. That's a pretty name," he finally said softly. He grabbed her hand and led her out of the fountain.

Esa followed him eagerly. *Now* was all that mattered, she told herself. Didn't she deserve a night of guilt-free, fantastic sex?

She'd deal with the inevitable damage come morning.

Chapter Seven

⌘

Her teeth were chattering by the time they reached Finn's air-conditioned building. Despite all the heat they'd generated in the park—and even in the backseat of the cab on the way to his condo—it struck Finn as he turned to face her after shutting his front door that Esa looked cold, wet and miserable as she stood there in his foyer.

And was that anxiety he saw shadowing her features? If he didn't keep an eye on her constantly she was going to bolt again, he realized grimly. He opened his lips to ask her what, precisely, she had against him for a bed partner when she suddenly spoke.

"*You're* the one who got me all wet," she said defensively, her brandy-colored eyes flashing fire.

Finn paused in surprise, mouth hanging open. She was such a damn *fickle* creature—purring one second and hissing at him the next.

"You were staring at me like you think I look like a drowned rat," she prevaricated when he shook his head in disgust.

"I was admiring your charms in a wet t-shirt actually. Has anybody ever told you you've got a mile-wide chip on your shoulder?" he demanded as he came toward her.

She mumbled something waspishly under her breath but the only thing he caught was *mostly just get that...stifling bore.*

"What did you say?" he asked as he stepped next to her and his arms encircled her waist.

She looked up...and just like that she switched on him again. Her eyes smoldered in invitation. Despite being witness to one of many of her bewildering flip-flops in mood, Finn felt his body responding to that sultry stare.

He'd be damned if she didn't possess the sexiest eyes he'd ever seen in his life. Her silky pale skin, long shapely legs, curvy hips, round ass, luminous smile—not to mention a chest that made him want to spend a solid week in bed with her—had Finn's cock twitching pretty much constantly when he was with her.

But her eyes were the stuff out of a man's dream.

He bent his knees and his arms tightened around her, bringing their groins and bellies flush against each other. He spread both hands over her round, damp fanny and rocked her against him.

"Why is it that I feel like the important things about you are the things you say under your breath, Esa?"

"Why is it that I feel the things you don't say at all are the things that are most important about you?" she countered quickly. "How much do you really need to know about me?"

He caressed her witchy grin with his lips. "The only thing I need to know at the moment is how your naked skin feels against mine."

"That sounds like a promising place to begin," she agreed before she delicately licked his lower lip. He let her play with him for a few seconds but when her taste fully registered in his awareness he sank his tongue into her sweetness.

He lifted his head a steam-filled twenty seconds later. "Let's go," he said before he urged her ahead of him in the direction of his bedroom. He unglued his eyes from her swaying ass, tightly covered in damp denim, when he realized that she was heading for the bed.

"Uh uh." He tugged on her hand. "You're cold and wet. I'm putting you in a hot bath."

"Oh? What are you going to do while I'm bathing?" she asked doubtfully. Her gaze flickered down to where his cock was practically bursting to get free of his button-fly.

He laughed. Obviously she didn't think the available evidence indicated that he'd be able to wait for long. He hoped she wasn't right, because he wanted to take his time with her. Finn couldn't remember being this aroused by a woman in a long time...maybe ever.

At that moment, he was *glad* that she drove a car that sent out a bold sexual invitation to half the population of the world...and likely then some. He was *ecstatic* that she considered what was between his thighs to be infinitely more important than what was between his ears.

In that second, he pretty much agreed with her.

But even if all she did want from him was a single night of sizzling sex, this time Finn was going to savor her.

"I'm the one who's going to be bathing you," he explained.

"Oh?" she asked, wide-eyed.

"Arms up," he prodded a few seconds later, after he'd turned the double taps, one on each end of the tub, on full force.

"This is an amazing bathroom," she said, her voice muffled by the fact that he pulled her damp t-shirt over her head. "Actually, the whole condo is amazing. I never...got a chance to tell you yesterday."

Finn smiled when he saw color brighten her cheeks. How was it possible that such an accomplished flirt and self-proclaimed man-eater blushed more than his sixteen-year-old sister Anna Jean when Jess teased her about the boys who called her? His gaze lowered over her elegant neck, dewy shoulders and generous breasts encased in a white lace bra. As he'd frequently had cause to appreciate over the course of the afternoon, the undergarment wasn't padded. He spied the rosy pink color of her nipples through the tight lace.

He grimaced slightly as he ripped open the top few buttons of his jeans to give him some breathing room. Christ.

Looking at her in that skimpy bra was like taking a slug of distilled, Grade-A, punch-in-the-gut lust.

Okay, so her proclivity to blush was about the *only* thing this incredibly sexy woman had in common with Anna Jean.

"Is something wrong?"

He blinked, realizing that he'd been gawking.

"No. Well…nothing except for the fact that I'm pissed off at myself for being in such a hurry that I didn't even take off your blouse last night," he added gruffly before he reached around and unfastened her bra. He ought to be shot for ignoring such bounty. He held his breath as he peeled the tight material off her breasts. When he finally exhaled he did so on a hiss.

"Damn, you're something to look at, Esa."

"Thank you," she whispered.

"Let's get you out of the rest of these wet clothes so we can work on getting you warmed up," he encouraged gently.

* * * * *

When every last wet stitch of her clothing lay rumpled on the white marble tile floor, Finn stepped closer to her. She felt the heat emanating off his aroused body.

"Your clothes are damp," she complained, despite the fact that she cuddled closer to him.

"Well, if you'd give me a chance I'd get naked too. Jeez, you're freezing, aren't you?"

Esa moaned in arousal when he began to rub the skin on her back, arms and hips briskly, warming her flesh in more ways than one.

"Oooh, get undressed so we can get in the tub," she begged, although she didn't even attempt to move away from his heat or his industrious hands moving all over her body. She looked up at him when he began rubbing her bare bottom. He paused for a second and then palmed the cheeks in a possessive gesture that made warm liquid pool between her thighs.

"It's going to be the challenge of a lifetime to go slow with you," he admitted softly.

"No need to go slow on my account."

He just chuckled and swatted her bottom. Esa jumped like the sound of flesh smacking against flesh had been a gunshot.

"Okay. The water's deep enough. Go ahead and get in," Finn said.

Esa bent over and checked the temperature of the water, purring when she felt the delicious heat. Finn's whirlpool tub was modeled after the old-fashioned standalone kind, although this was deeper and large enough for two, in addition to having two steps that encircled the interior.

The entire bathroom was another example of tasteful luxury. It was larger than Esa's second bedroom in her condo.

She looked over her shoulder to ask him whether his ex-fiancée or he himself had decorated the condo when she noticed how rigid his handsome face looked. She stood abruptly, realizing that she was bending over the tub with her bare butt in the air.

"Aren't you coming?" she asked in an unnaturally high-pitched voice as she stepped into the deep tub.

"Absolutely. Hopefully several times."

She rolled her eyes at his double entendre.

He grinned as he came toward her and switched on the whirlpool jets. "I told you I was going to bathe you. Then maybe I'll join you."

Esa sighed in pure bliss when she finally leaned back in the frothing water. "Heaven," she whispered as her eyes closed. But she was too excited to remain in repose for long. The last thing she felt like doing when she was buck naked and Finn Madigan was in the room with her was fall asleep.

Her family and friends might think she was lame but she wasn't a fool.

Not by a mile, Esa added to herself as she watched Finn pull over a stool. He retrieved a thick white towel and a loofah from a linen closet and set them down on the stool.

"You weren't serious about bathing me."

"Do you have anything to hold up your hair?"

"Uh...yes, there's a clip in my backpack, I think," Esa muttered dubiously.

"I'll be right back."

She moved restlessly in the bubbling water when Finn returned and immediately scooped up her hair, fixing it into what Esa was confident was a haphazard mess upon her head. He whipped off his outer shirt and tossed it aside before turning off both taps. He sat down behind her head and picked up a thick bar of soap.

"This really isn't necessary," Esa protested weakly when he began to lather up her shoulders and chest. His hands were slightly roughened by calluses. They felt delicious against her smooth, wet skin. He alternated between massaging her shoulder and neck muscles deeply and merely gliding his fingertips along the sensitive surfaces.

"What's wrong? Not used to being pampered, is that it?" he taunted in a low, resonant voice that made the hairs on the back of her exposed neck stand on end. He was right, of course. She'd never had a lover—especially such a beautiful one—treat her like she was a queen.

Esa wasn't sure if she should allow herself to enjoy the delicious sensations coursing through her body. She'd always had to struggle a bit to "let go" during sex, always feeling like she owed her lover something extra in bed because she wasn't model-thin and photo-ready for the cover of *Cosmo*. Not that her handful of past lovers had necessarily been ready for the covers of *GQ* either but...

Well, it was a man's world after all.

Flirting in Traffic

She soon discovered that Finn wasn't leaving her a choice about giving in completely to her desire about utterly giving in to *him*. He turned off the jets of the whirlpool and told her to rise up onto the deepest step of the tub. "Lean forward," he directed.

She sat in the waist-deep water while he lathered up her back, massaging her until her flesh melted beneath the influence of the heat and his skilled hands.

She groaned when he transferred to using the loofah, gently abrading her flushed skin.

"You're not pampering me, you're spoiling me," she murmured.

He chuckled while he rinsed off her back. Esa wondered with mild amusement if she even possessed a backbone a few minutes later when he put both hands on her shoulders and she sank back onto the edge of the tub.

"*Ohhh*," she moaned when his hands suddenly were cradling her breasts, shaping the flesh in his large palms, massaging the beading nipples between soap-slick fingertips. Her hips squirmed in arousal.

"See? I have good motivation for spoiling you," he rasped near her ear. The manner in which he played with her breasts and teased and plucked at her nipples, with such focused intent, left Esa speechless with desire. For a prolonged moment of unbearable tension he learned her shape and texture, determining precisely which caresses evoked whimpers of longing from her throat, always refining his attack until Esa was sure she could take no more.

Her head fell back helplessly onto his hard thigh.

"Take me to bed," she pleaded. She almost screamed in protest when he removed his hands from her breasts.

"In a moment. I can't finish bathing you unless I get in there with you."

When she glanced around and saw him whipping his white t-shirt over his head, Esa forgot about protesting. Her mouth went dry at the sudden appearance of the breathtaking masculine landscape before her, consisting of flexing, ridged muscle and golden-brown skin. She followed the hasty movements of his fingers on his fly hungrily. She bit her lower lip hard in order to suppress an agonized groan when his penis sprang free of his jeans and boxer briefs.

Oh my.

Her memory certainly hadn't led her astray. He truly was every bit as beautiful as she recalled from their too-brief encounter last night.

More so.

She giggled when he rambunctiously clambered into the tub, splashing water over the sides. "Let out some of the water! You're too big. It's getting all over the floor."

"So? It'll dry." He dropped to his knees in the tub and reached for her. Esa howled in laughter when he tickled her belly and waist. More water sloshed out of the tub in the tussle that followed.

"Stop…*oh*…stop it, Finn! I'm extremely ticklish."

"I noticed," Finn said with an evil, lecherous grin. By the time he finished tickling her Esa was gasping for breath between jags of laughter and there was more water on the floor than in the tub.

"Okay, I've tortured you enough for now," Finn proclaimed before he dropped a warm kiss on her parted lips. Her desperate pants for air utterly ceased when he sandwiched his hand between her clenched thighs and pressed upward, applying a steady pressure on her already hyperaroused sex. "Now you get a reward for putting up with my teasing."

All remnants of mirth faded from her consciousness. "A-a reward?"

"Uh huh," he replied silkily. "You've warmed up enough now, aren't you? Scoot up onto the next step."

Warm didn't begin to describe Esa's temperature as Finn placed his hands on her bare hips and urged her higher in the water until only her legs were submerged. When he picked up the large bar of yellow soap and begin to lather up his hands, her thighs clamped back together to alleviate the unbearable throb of anticipation at their apex.

"Stay spread while I wash your legs," Finn demanded. Esa just stared, completely ensnared in a sensual haze as he lifted each of her legs out of the water in turn and washed and caressed every inch of them. She groaned in agonized pleasure when he treated each foot to a deep massage. The man's hands were a gift from God, there was no doubt about it.

After he'd rinsed her second leg and foot completely, he transferred his attentions to her hips, rubbing the bar of soap directly on her skin and following with a circling palm and splashes of warm water. Esa whimpered softly when he gently spread her thighs further apart and slid the slippery hard surface of the soap down through her damp pubic hair.

He pushed her legs closed and continued to manipulate the bar of soap up and down between her clasping thighs.

"*Finn.*" She grabbed onto his shoulders desperately. He'd kissed and played with and teased her helpless flesh for so long now that she trembled in incipient release. He continued to press and lather the slick soap against her sensitive tissues, creating an eye-crossing pressure.

"Shhh," he soothed, even though he denied her the slightest opportunity for calming down by replacing the soap with his fingers, lowering his golden head and slipping a nipple into his mouth.

Esa came so violently that she checked out of reality for a few seconds.

When she came back to herself he still stroked her intimately, causing delicious aftershocks of pleasure to ripple through her body. But he was no longer sucking on her nipple. Instead he watched her through narrow slits of fiery topaz.

"All warmed up now?" he rasped.

The explosion of pleasure that had just rocked her world had temporarily deprived her energy to speak so she just nodded.

"Good. Then it's time for bed now, Esa."

Chapter Eight

Finn kept forcefully directing his brain onto one thing and one thing only—taking his time with Esa. The interest—or *ability* for that matter—to question logically why he should be so dead set on the challenge had long fled him.

Unfortunately, the organ that dominated almost his entire awareness as he carried her to his bed wasn't remotely interested in logic.

He grunted as he came down on the mattress and hauled an armful of fragrant, wet, delicious woman on top of him. He scooted back on the cool duvet cover until he leaned partially against the pillows and the padded headboard.

It pleased him beyond measure to know that Esa was doing the precise opposite of bolting at present. In fact she was all over him, running her hands hungrily over his body, scraping her nails lightly against his sides, making his skin roughen with goose bumps.

Not to mention that she kissed him with such desperate abandon that Finn temporarily knew only the primitive male mandate to mate...and fast and furiously, at that. The firecracker was back in his arms again and damned if she wasn't taking him along with her once again on a wild, explosive ride.

He managed to break their kiss with a supreme effort of will.

"Esa, stop a moment," he growled, desire making him hoarse.

She glanced up at him from his chest where she had been tonguing and nibbling his nipples. Even though he'd just asked her to stop, Finn forced himself to resist an almost overwhelming urge to push her head back down.

"You made me feel so good. I want to return the favor," she said softly.

"Esa," he grated out when she fisted his aching cock. He refused to let her turn him inside out all over again.

But the moment she bent at the waist and added her gliding tongue and wet, suctioning mouth to the scenario, Finn's restraint vaporized for the second time in two nights.

Her hand lowered to the root of his cock, holding him at her mercy as she explored him. His entire body went rigid, every cell of his being seemingly focused on the movement of her searching tongue, her tight lips, her sweet, hungry suck.

When her head moved over his lap faster and more forcefully he groaned gutturally, his pleasure building way too quickly for his liking. His hands fisted her thick hair. Despite his attempts at restraint, he was unable to stop himself from lifting his hips, giving himself to her when she was willing to take him so greedily.

"*Stop.* Come here," he demanded after a moment in a much harder voice than he'd intended.

She looked up from his lap. The sight of her huge, brandy-colored eyes clouded with desire and her damp, lush lips just inches from his straining cock almost sent him over the edge. He momentarily stilled the urge by focusing on the task of retrieving a condom from his bedside table.

She straddled his lap as he ripped open the packaging. He grimaced in pleasure at the sensation of her sliding his near-to-bursting erection between the silky, firm globes of her ass cheeks. It was bad enough that she had an ass that could turn a man into a rutting beast but she made matters worse by rubbing it against him when he was near to bursting.

And purring.

He stilled her squirming hips, furious at her for teasing him so mercilessly.

"If you don't hold still I'm gonna paddle your sweet ass."

She laughed, calling his bluff. The low, husky sound of her mirth was almost as potent as her squirming on his cock had been. He couldn't take another second. He tightened the hold on her hips, urging her to take him inside the humid heat that emanated from her core into his skin.

When she slid down over him, tentatively at first then with one downward surge of her hips, a rough growl scored his throat. Was everything she did merciless? She squeezed him in a tight, warm fist. He pressed down on her waist, silently begging her not to move until he regained control.

She panted shallowly. She leaned forward and drew little circles with her hips, biting her lower lip and moaning in pleasure.

"Christ, you're incorrigible," Finn grated out, leaning forward and holding her more tightly onto his lap. He found himself within inches of her large, shapely breasts capped by erect, dark pink nipples.

He swallowed thickly, feeling himself jerk inside of her tight, clasping sheath. He leaned back into the headboard, aware that sweat was pouring off him.

"I'm sorry, Finn."

"You don't look like it, Esa," he muttered wryly as he eyed her bewitching little smile.

Her eyes went wide when he said her name. She shifted her hips forward on him again, ever so slightly. He knew where she was seeking relief and he reached for her, offering it with his massaging thumb. He couldn't help but smirk in profound satisfaction when she writhed against him and her sleek channel tightened around his cock.

"Two can play at torture," he reminded her. He became increasingly aware, however, that his desire to make her squirm a little was making her do just that, flinging his challenge back in his own face. Her restless, gripping movements around his cock drove him wild.

Esa paused a moment, gulping for air. His circling thumb sent her straight into blissful orbit. She burned. Everywhere—the soles of her feet, her aching nipples...but mostly beneath Finn's magical finger. The pressure he applied was cruel in its perfection. She leaned forward and placed her hands on his hard, hair-dusted chest. She moved her hips in tight, gyrating movements.

Finn snarled. His fingers sank into the soft, firm flesh of her ass cheek, encouraging her to ride him.

"Oh, Oh...*yes*!" Esa shouted when he finally let her have her way and she hopped in his lap, stroking him fierce and fast. When Finn increased the rate of his circling thumb, she yelped helplessly and tipped over into climax.

Finn held her to him while she came, one hand splayed across her stomach, reaching down to the sensitive flesh where he nursed her through her orgasm, the other firmly holding her down, motionless, on his cock. He inhaled deeply, struggling for one last ounce of control as her clasping channel spasmed and pulled at his straining cock.

She sagged against his chest. Finn flexed his abdominal muscles and straightened his back slightly, fully supporting them on the headboard. He urged her back up to a sitting position.

He wanted her beautiful breasts directly in front of his face when he came.

While she panted and recovered from her orgasm he leaned forward at his leisure and nuzzled the bountiful glory before him with his nose and lips before he slid a hard little bud between his lips. She whimpered and tightened around him.

He groaned.

"You have the most incredible breasts," he murmured as he moved his head between both of them, licking, sipping, nibbling and sucking, mindlessly ecstatic at the feast before him.

He demanded that she move on him again, this time adding the strength of his hips and upper body, pushing her down on his cock in short, staccato thrusts that made both of them cry out in pleasure.

Esa became lost once again in the web of mindless carnality that Finn spun so effortlessly around her. She sensed the tension mounting in him, felt it in the bulging tightness of his chest, arm and thigh muscles. He completely controlled her movements now, lifting and thrusting the weight of her body down on him with a breathtaking force that she'd been unable to accomplish on her own.

She cried out sharply when he brought her down forcefully one last time, their flesh smacking together loudly.

He held her down in his lap. His handsome face contorted into a rictus of pleasure.

"*Esa.*"

She cried out sharply, the moment made perfect by hearing her name on his tongue at his moment of crisis.

She felt him spasm deep inside of her. As he held her to him his mouth fastened on her right nipple, drawing on her lustily while he shuddered in orgasm. The sensation sizzled like lightning straight to her core. She ground down on the stiff pillar of his convulsing cock, climaxing again with shattering intensity.

For several minutes, the only sound in the room was that of their heavy breathing as they desperately tried to gain equilibrium.

Esa lay on his chest, wilted, warm and utterly replete. She lightly placed her hands on his sweat-dampened rib cage, feeling it rise up and down as his breathing evened and deepened. With her head turned on his chest she could hear his heartbeat, strong, regular and gradually slowing.

She felt poignantly attuned with Finn as she lay there, as if their bodily processes had synchronized, their flesh separate but somehow unified. When he withdrew from her body she wanted to cry out in protest. But soon enough he'd pulled her down next to his hard, warm length again. He burrowed his fingers into her hair, rubbing her scalp.

Esa purred in contentment.

"Hey," he murmured with quiet amusement. "Look what I found."

"What?" she asked groggily, lifting her head from his chest. She blinked, trying to focus on what he held up between his fingers in the dim room, which was illuminated only by the bathroom light. After a few seconds she chuckled in recognition.

"It's a leaf. I raked my parents' backyard today," she said before she dropped her cheek back to his chest.

"Where do they live?" he asked in a low, mellow tone that Esa loved.

"Evanston, right off Lake Shore Drive in the house I grew up in."

"I thought you said you'd lived in Chicago your whole life."

"I did. You're not that meticulous about your definitions, are you?"

"Right," he agreed wryly. "Chicago, Evanston…Esa, Kitten. No one could claim that you're loose in your interpretations."

She grinned into his chest, appreciating his humor but not being in a position to show it because of her chosen role. Her smile faded a bit. She hoped he hadn't been insinuating she was loose in general…

"Kitten is a-a—"

"Pet name?"

She lifted her head and stared at his face. She snorted with laughter when she saw the mirthful gleam in his eyes.

"I went to school in Chicago until I graduated high school. Doesn't that count for anything?" Esa asked eventually, thinking it was best to stick to a topic that didn't require lying.

"Which one?"

"The Latin School."

"Hmmm."

"What's that supposed to mean?"

"Nothing." He began his delicious scalp rub again but Esa wouldn't be sidetracked. He grinned when he saw her challenging look.

"The Latin School is a rich kid's school," he explained matter-of-factly.

"It is not!"

Finn shrugged negligently, as though the matter was beneath his notice.

"My father is a professor and my mother is a real estate agent. We were hardly rich. Why? Where did you go to school?"

"St. Mark's."

"Ah hah!" she said with a triumphant look. "You went to a private school as well."

"Catholic school. Not remotely the same."

"Did you go to college?" Esa asked.

"Yep. A four-year one with a real campus and everything."

Esa stilled with wariness when she registered the subtle mockery of his tone. "Where at?" she asked, refusing to be cowed by his entirely uncalled-for testiness.

"The University of Illinois," he replied after a pause. "Okay, time for you to answer a question for me."

Esa stilled warily. "What?"

"Why were you driving north in traffic yesterday when your offices are downtown?"

"Oh, well that's because..." Esa paused, licking her lower lip nervously. This would probably be a good time to tell him that she wasn't *Metro Sexy's* publisher. But she felt foolish for having lied about it in the first place and besides...he'd made it clear that he wasn't interested in anything permanent. It was clear from his occasional prickliness in regard to matters that had nothing to do with Esa that he was still very much in the jittery aftershocks of a bad break-up.

No call for her to turn back from her impulsive adventure now.

Her mind scrambled for work activities that she'd heard Rachel mention in the past. She finally landed on her sister's real reason for being in Indianapolis for the next week and conveniently changed locations. "I've been having some meetings about possibly doing a...a...South Side version of *Metro Sexy*."

Finn looked puzzled.

"You know, a version that's just for single southsiders — where to eat, good nightclubs, social events..."

"Hmmm," Finn muttered.

Esa heard the doubt in his tone.

"What's wrong?" she demanded. Part of her laughed at herself for being offended that he didn't think her idea for a job that she knew absolutely nothing about was an ingenious marketing plan.

He shrugged. "I don't know anything about publishing but it just doesn't sound like something the typical Chicago southsider would go for. We're a more...practical lot."

Esa chuckled and snuggled back into his warmth. She perfectly saw his point, so she thought it best to put an end to the subject.

Or the lie, to be more accurate.

His arms encircled her and tightened. A small smile curved her lips. God, she could die a happy woman lying here in Finn's embrace and inhaling his scent.

Her eyes flashed open. What a bizarre—not to mention dangerous—thought.

Finn paused when he felt her stiffen in his arms. "What's wrong?"

"Nothing."

She yelped in surprise when he spun her onto her back and rolled on top of her in two seconds flat.

"You're a liar, Esa Ormond."

Her eyes went wide at his stark accusation and the abrupt change of her circumstances. Her heartbeat began to pound out a warning in her ears. His eyelids narrowed. The seconds stretched unbearably long as Finn subjected her to his laserlike inspection.

He finally sighed and shook his head slowly. "I'd sure like to know why you get so defensive sometimes."

She gasped in surprise. "Talk about calling a kettle black! You're the one who got so prickly about that college thing."

"Guess you subscribe to the best offense is a consistent defense theory of combat?"

"I don't want to *fight* with you," she sputtered incredulously.

He grimaced slightly. "Sorry. I was doing it again, wasn't I?"

Esa just raised her eyebrows wryly. "Nice of you to realize who was in bed with you. Let me guess. Your ex-fiancée wasn't only snooty when it came to things like where you worked but where you went to school as well."

She went completely still when he leaned down over her until his lips almost brushed her own. "I don't really feel like talking about that right now. Do you?"

He dropped a slow kiss on her upturned lips. It was a closed-mouth kiss—nowhere near as blatantly sexual as he'd kissed her in the past—but Esa found herself wondering if it wasn't the most erotic kiss of all. He sandwiched first her lower lip between his own, then the upper. He rubbed against her and molded and teased until she squirmed beneath him in renewed arousal.

"I'll take that as a *no*," he said huskily before he applied those gold-medal lips to her neck. She shivered.

"W-what?" she asked, no longer certain what they'd been talking about.

He examined her face before he smiled.

"Never mind. I'm about to make love to you again," he explained patiently. "Are you going to be good?"

"What do you mean?" she asked suspiciously.

"I mean that if you don't hold still while my tongue familiarizes itself with every inch of your beautiful body, I'm going to have to tie you down to this bed."

"You would never do that," Esa scoffed. She paused, mouth hanging open, when she saw the gleam in his blue eyes and felt his cock lengthen and stiffen against her thigh. He didn't bother to reply but just lowered his head and proceeded to make good on his threat.

She gasped at the sensation of his firm lips and warm, slightly abrasive tongue on her shoulder. He took a gentle bite out of the muscle before he scraped his front teeth along her neck.

Esa tried her best to keep still but she couldn't seem to stop from arching her back, suddenly desperate to rub her hypersensitive nipples against the crinkly hair on his chest.

He'd said her body was *beautiful*. Was it remotely possible that Finn didn't mind that she hadn't been to the gym in almost a year and staged a daily battle with the Häagen-Dazs cookie dough ice cream in her freezer...a battle which she usually lost miserably? She ground her teeth together and forced herself to remain stationary when he kissed the sensitive sides of her torso and examined her goose bumps with his sleek tongue.

She would persevere at all costs, excruciating torture though it would be.

Chapter Nine

Finn lay in bed, lazy and extremely sated, while he watched dawn break around Esa where she stood by the windows. He found himself entranced by her still figure, the beguiling, feminine curve of her hip, the contemplative tilt of her head, the elegant lines of her back.

When she'd come out of the bathroom a few minutes ago she'd been wearing his discarded gray flannel work shirt. It fell on her to mid-thigh, leaving exposed a good portion of her long, shapely legs. She'd brushed her hair while she'd been in there because it hung below her shoulders in shiny auburn waves.

He'd wager that most women would be extremely envious of Esa's natural beauty. She'd awaken after only an hour or two or actual sleep looking downright gorgeous—skin glowing, hair mussed and spilling in a sexy auburn mess around her lovely face...the mysterious smile of a well-satisfied woman on her swollen, well-kissed lips, Finn added to himself with a touch of male smugness.

He had no grounds for being cocky, of course. She was the most sensual, responsive, carnal creature he'd ever had the privilege to make love to, and that had precious little to do with him. But it wasn't only her sexuality that had captivated him throughout the long night. So had her obvious intelligence, her sense of humor...even the occasional glimpses of her little insecurities.

He liked Esa Ormond—he liked her a lot. Too bad he'd met her at such a crappy time in his life.

His eyelids narrowed on her thoughtful feminine form outlined by the sunrise. It wasn't just his recent breakup that made a relationship between them highly unlikely. Esa had clearly stated that she wasn't looking for anything permanent. She was obviously used to having casual affairs, given the circumstances of how they'd met and her job. Which was convenient for him.

Wasn't it?

He frowned.

"Come back to bed," he called, eager to chase away his unsettling thoughts.

She turned and gave him a smile that made his demand even more imperative. "I have a better idea."

He shook his head while he held her stare. "Ain't a conceivable better idea in the entire world, honey. Come here."

She laughed low and husky as she came toward him. "Even you can't have that much energy. Come on, get out of bed. You'll like this, I promise."

He couldn't resist the sparkle in her brandy-colored eyes.

"How long will I have to be out of bed?" he asked warily.

"An hour, tops," she answered as she pulled the comforter and sheet off him. He caught it and yanked tautly to garner her attention.

"On one condition."

Her dark eyebrows rose expectantly.

"We get right back in bed the minute we get back."

She lowered her eyes and trailed her gaze down his naked torso. Despite their multiple rounds of sometimes fierce, sometimes playful, always intense lovemaking, Finn found himself stiffening beneath the sheets once again.

From the look of her widening smile she'd noticed.

"You really do have enough energy, don't you?" she mused a tad incredulously. She shook her head as though to clear it and resumed pulling on the sheet. "All right, then. You have yourself a deal."

"Where are we going?" he asked when Esa merged onto Lakeshore Drive. She'd insisted that there wasn't time to shower. They'd just thrown on their clothes and hurried to Esa's little sports car as if a sudden emergency had been broadcast to her while she stared out his bedroom window not ten minutes ago.

"*Here*," she responded as she shifted gears and the car accelerated forward like a jet.

"Here?" he repeated as he glanced at the four lanes of Lake Shore Drive. The stretch of relatively empty road must have been what she'd seen from his bedroom window. Lake Shore Drive offered a beautiful view of the lake and Chicago's skyline but it was almost always crowded with cars. Esa had seen her opportunity to drive fast and free and grabbed it, Finn realized with mixed admiration and amusement.

The sun sat like a giant orange ball on the horizon. Lake Michigan rippled calmly, its color a muted steel blue. Esa had put back the top on her sports car before they'd left his parking garage. The early morning autumn air felt cool but pleasant as it whipped through his hair.

He studied Esa as she drove. She had on the preppy glasses she always wore driving. He thought she looked sexy as hell in them, although he liked her without them just as much since it gave him more direct access to her warm, brandy-colored eyes. She'd clipped her hair onto her head but auburn strands still lashed wildly around her cheeks and neck as she drove. She seemed unaware of it.

She looked sublimely content as she hurtled down the miraculously empty ribbon of curving road, the sun rising over the lake on the right and the high-rises towering over them to the left, the tall buildings seeming sober and watchful in the early morning light.

Neither of them spoke until she parked in the empty lot at the Montrose beach.

"You really love it, don't you?" he asked after they got out and sat on a picnic table, watching the sun begin its slow ascent.

"The lake?" she asked.

"No. Driving that car."

She laughed. "I don't know. I never thought about it before. I suppose I do. Maybe I've been driving in traffic too much lately. There's something freeing about an open stretch of road."

"And a fast car," he added with amusement.

She shot him a look of reprimand. "I'm not actually into fast, flashy cars."

"Uh-huh," he murmured doubtfully while he tucked an errant tress of auburn hair behind her ear.

Her big eyes widened. "You don't believe me?"

"Why should I, when all evidence points to the contrary? A, you do, in fact, own an expensive, fast car; B, I was getting a little jealous of a the damned thing for putting a look on your face that I've only seen so far after a round of great sex, and C...you're extremely good at it."

"At sex?" she asked dazedly.

"No," he replied. He chuckled when her transfixed expression changed to irritability quicker than he could say, *damn*. He came down off the picnic table and gathered her into his arms. "I was talking about your driving. Rest assured, your talent and enthusiasm for driving nearly matches your proclivities in the bedroom. I stress, *nearly*."

When she appeared pacified but still bemused he brushed his lips against her parted ones.

"Nobody has ever told me I was a great...driver before," she mumbled against his mouth.

"Well, you are," he assured her, letting his lips caress hers as he spoke. "An exciting, skilled...extremely *precise* driver."

He kissed her once, hard, before he briefly lifted his head. "For my sake though, I wish you'd slow down some."

"What's the fun in that?" she whispered before she craned up and touched her grin to his.

They kissed warmly, playfully. That was one thing he really liked about Esa—how easy it was to play with her sexually, how lighthearted and *good* it felt at times.

It felt like precisely what he needed at this point in his life.

As he'd quickly learned was the usual case with Esa, however, what began as teasing and playful became hot and eye-crossingly serious in no time flat. She tasted like mint mouthwash with just a hint of cherry that had nothing to do with the plastic bottle of green fluid in his bathroom and everything to do with Esa's singular taste. She smelled like fresh air and sweet, well-loved woman.

He thought of what she'd tasted like when he'd finally coated his tongue in her honeyed, musky essence last night.

His cock swelled hard and full at the thought of tasting her again, the strength and near-pain of his body's reaction shocking him a little.

"How fast do you think you can get us back to bed, Speed Racer?"

"We're there within ten minutes," Esa replied huskily.

"Make it eight and I'll give you a prize."

Her eyes smoldered. "And if I make it seven?"

"I'll make it the grand one," he promised as he grabbed her hand and they jogged toward the car.

He seriously considered doing a rerun of their foyer escapade from a few nights ago when she yanked him down to her like some kind of lusty barbarian warrior-queen the second after he closed his front door. But no, he'd learned his lesson. What if this was the last time he made love to her?

He'd take her right...no matter how much she tempted him.

He chuckled into her ravenous kiss even though amusement wasn't his only reaction to his thoughts. Lust was the other. What man wouldn't want to be ravaged by a fiery red-haired beauty who was built along the lines of Wonder Woman, a la Lynda Carter?

What red-blooded man wouldn't want to tame the little hellion?

Okay, maybe she wasn't *little* relative to other women, Finn thought as he overfilled his hand with a firm breast, but she was little compared to him. Graceful and delightfully curved, not to mention the most exciting woman he'd ever kept sequestered in his bed for a night of pleasure.

For a morning of it.

For an afternoon and evening, if he could talk her into it.

He tripped over her feet as he returned her kiss with equal ravenous hunger and pushed her back to his bedroom.

They finally stumbled and fell on his bed in a tangle of long limbs and craning necks. She tried to roll on top of him but he held her down with ease with his flexing, spread thighs and heavier weight.

She squirmed beneath him.

"Are you that anxious for your prize?" he asked with gruff amusement as he ground his cock in the heat emanating from the apex of her thighs. She resisted the pressure with her hips, rubbing up against him like a strong, supple feline in heat.

"You know I am, you damned—"

She paused in the process of biting his lower lip between her small white teeth when the sound of a key in the front door lock penetrated the cloud of thick lust that surrounded them.

"*Shit*," Finn muttered with blistering heat.

It must be building maintenance. Was there something elementally wrong with his condo that he hadn't had the ability to notice with his nose next to Esa's fragrant skin? Was the building perhaps going up in flames around him while he operated under the sole dictate to bury himself between her thighs?

"Who's *there*?" he roared. His head reared up. He was furious with *anything* that even remotely dared to interfere with his possession of the warm, vibrant, succulent female he held captive beneath his body. A second later he heard a voice call out his name and a familiar figure walked through the door of his bedroom.

Not an inferno then. More like an earthquake.

"Julia. What the *hell* are you doing here?"

* * * * *

Esa pushed on Finn's chest in a silent plea. Without removing his eyes from the stunning brunette who had just walked into his room wearing a black and white formal gown, cashmere wrap and large diamonds in her ears and around her elegant throat, Finn stood up at the side of the bed.

Esa clambered up after him, all too eager to not be left lying on the bed with her legs spread wide in front of this divine creature who currently watched her with an impassive stare tinged with dark amusement.

"I apologize. I'd not realized you were entertaining a guest. How are you, Esa?"

"Just dandy, Julia," Esa answered while she shot a fulminating look at Finn.

He stared first at her, then at Julia, then back at Esa, as though he were convinced he was hallucinating current events.

"You two *know* each other?" he asked incredulously.

Julia gave a small, elegant shrug. "We know each other from our Junior League days."

"Still partying until dawn I see," Esa said scathingly as her eyes swept down the woman's slender, *Town & Country*-cover-ready figure. Her voice sounded cool but in truth her heart beat frantically in her ears.

"I attended a charity ball last night to benefit St. Jude's Children's Hospital. Unfortunately my date is passed out cold in our hotel room. Gavin likes his drink a bit too much."

Esa's jaw dropped in disbelief when she saw the way Julia gave Finn a smoky look as though Esa wasn't even in the room.

What the *hell* was Julia Weatherell—the only woman who held a viable claim to her sister Rachel's title as the reigning social queen of Chicago—doing in Finn's condo looking like she owned the place and treating Esa as if she were some small annoyance, like a suspicious-looking spot on the carpet? Of course Esa knew the answer, impossible though it seemed.

Shit. If this didn't beat all. *Julia Weatherell* was Finn's ex-fiancée?

"Finn? May I have a word?" Julia asked in that low, cigarette-rough voice that Esa used to hate...and envy like crazy. It only made her more jealous that Julia possessed that sexy voice without ever touching a cigarette.

Finn met Esa's eyes briefly before he grimly nodded at the bedroom door and followed Julia out of the room. He pulled the door closed behind them, but not all the way.

And Esa was so wild with curiosity at that moment she wasn't above listening in through the crack.

"Give me the key," she heard Finn say clearly in a low, furious tone.

The sound of keys jangling on a keychain and Julia's husky laughter filtered in through the door. She imagined Julia dropping the key into his waiting palm in the silence that followed, letting her fingertips linger on his skin the process.

Esa's lungs began to burn as she waited in trepidation and forgot to breathe.

"I like that new vase. Did you get it from Serge at Mycroft and Sons? It would look better over on the credenza next to the bowl that we bought together in Paris. Remember that little restaurant next to the shop where we found it? And how after we drank almost two bottles of wine we went back to the hotel room and—"

"What the *hell* are you doing here?" Finn interrupted, the degree of rage in his tone highly gratifying to Esa.

Or maybe it shouldn't be gratifying? Would he be so royally pissed off if the gorgeous Julia didn't still have her hooks in him? Who was Esa kidding? She knew too much about Julia Weatherell to think it was possible for a man to become impervious to her charms.

Besides, hadn't Finn said they'd only broken up a month ago?

Finn and *Julia?* What a bizarre pairing. Julia was known for her snobbishness and Finn was one of the most down-to-earth people she'd ever met.

Once Julia had started a rumor about Rachel and Esa—one of many, at least in regards to Rachel—insinuating that neither of them really had attended college at Northwestern. Esa couldn't have cared less about Julia's petty rumor-mongering on the social circuit but Rachel had been in the process of acquiring investors to start up *Metro Sexy*. Her sister had nearly lost two crucial but wavering investors due to Julia's lies.

"I made a terrible mistake, Finn," Esa heard Julia say. "You should be glad to know that I'm being punished cruelly for my stupidity. I'm miserable. You have no idea how much I've regretted—"

Her voice broke with tears. Esa's eyes widened in panic at the sound. A beautiful, delicate creature like Julia was always a threat...but Julia vulnerable and overcome by emotion?

Don't even think about it.

"There are nights I would give anything, *do* anything to be back with you here in our cozy home," Julia muttered wetly.

Please, laying it on a bit thick aren't you, Julia? Esa thought with rising disbelief. Had she no shame? Surely Finn wasn't buying into this!

More soft crying and helpless hicupping ensued, only to be followed by a dreadful silence.

Some kind of masochistic urge made Esa press closer to the door. Oh God, *what* was going on out there? *Why aren't they speaking?* she wondered in rising panic. Surely it wasn't because they were experiencing a passionate, torrid clinch, was it?

Finally she heard Finn exhale audibly.

Don't let her pull you in, don't let her, Finn. Esa knew her mental chants had been for naught when she heard the softened quality of his deep voice when he spoke.

"I'm sorry you regret it, Julia. But—"

"Are you really?"

"Of course I am. I don't get off on the idea of you being unhappy. We were engaged for Christ's sake. I was in—"

He stopped abruptly.

Esa's heart plummeted into her stomach. Oh *no,* this was much, much worse than she'd suspected.

"You were the only one who really understood me, Finn. The only one who knew the *real* me."

"You made your choice. You can't come waltzing into this condo like you still live here. What's between us is over," he replied gently.

Damn straight it is, Esa thought.

"Is it, Finn? Is it really?" Julia asked tremulously.

Esa cringed in the silence that followed.

"Yes," Finn finally said.

Esa stepped back from the door. Never mind the single word that came out of Finn's mouth. That pregnant pause before he'd spoken had said it all.

She caught a glimpse of herself in the bathroom mirror when she rose from picking up her backpack. Her clothing was rumpled and smelled vaguely of mildew after sitting on Finn's damp bathroom floor all night. Her hair looked like a rat's nest.

And why the hell were there tears in her eyes? What kind of a pitiful fool was she to get emotional over a weekend fling, especially when the guy was clearly still pining for his gorgeous, deceitful ex-fiancée?

He must be a moron for getting involved with Julia Weatherell.

Except that she knew very well that Finn was far from being a moron. Esa had been firsthand witness to several of the brightest, sweetest guys in the city falling like lead for Julia. She was the kind of beautiful that made guys lose all remnants of rationality. Plus she was a savvy, sophisticated lawyer. Esa recalled that she was a successful Assistant United States Attorney General.

She was also poison, but apparently a sweet, addictive one when it came to men.

"I'll just let myself out," Esa proclaimed too brightly when she walked out of the bedroom a few seconds later.

She caught a glimpse of Julia's tear-stained, incredulous face. She didn't give herself time to interpret Finn's rigid expression before she raced for the door.

She stared blankly at the blurry reflection of herself in the gold elevator doors as they silently shut. Undoubtedly Finn had gotten his fill of her because this time he hadn't uttered a peep of protest about her abrupt departure.

Chapter Ten

Esa barely stopped herself from screaming like a blonde in a slasher movie when Mrs. Fuentes dug her cane between two bones in Esa's foot.

"Oh, I'm so sorry, Dr. Ormond!"

"It's okay," Esa grunted through a twisted grimace. "The elevator is always crowded on Fridays. I probably should have taken the stairs."

"Especially tonight. It's Halloween, you know. There's a party in the dining room," Mrs. Fuentes explained as Esa continued to grit her teeth as the pain in her foot ebbed from a roar to a dull throb.

"You're coming, aren't you, Dr. Ormond? I've got a bottle of gin for the punch and they're gonna show *Halloween 3*," Mortimer Shively provoked her with a sly grin.

Esa knew precisely which activity he expected her to lecture him about so she chose the other. "You better watch out, Mort. *Halloween 3* won't do your kidneys any favors either."

Mort snorted with laughter.

"*Look* at her, Shively. She's gorgeous. Why the heck would the doc want to party with a bunch of half-dead zombies like us?" Mr. Abercrombie growled.

"You know as well as I do I like going to Shady Lawn parties once in awhile, Mr. Abercrombie." Her brow crinkled in suspicion when she noticed Abercrombie's wry, assessing glance as he peered up at her from beneath bushy gray eyebrows. For some reason it reminded Esa of what Carla said last week about her reserving her room at Shady Lawn nursing home before she turned thirty.

One of the many things Carla had said in order to goad her into going to One Life.

Had it really been a whole week since she'd first seen Finn walk out of that construction trailer, six days since she'd stormed out of his condo and left him alone with that man-eater Julia Graves? She hadn't heard a whisper from him since. Now that the weekend was here, it seemed more and more unlikely that she'd ever hear from him again.

She was a fool for expecting anything different, of course. Hadn't they set clear parameters for their fling? He'd said he wanted his fill of her and surely she'd given it to him during that night of wild, uninhibited, write-to-*Cosmo*-it-was-so-phenomenal sex.

She'd been meticulous about driving Rachel's car in the far right lanes when they neared 63rd Street all week long, determinedly ignoring Carla's muttering under her breath that she was a coward in addition to being lame. Look where listening to her best friend had gotten her last week, after all?

Naked, shameless and lust-drunk beneath Finn Madigan's beautiful body, that's where.

She flinched away from Mrs. Fuentes' cane when the elevator door opened on the fifth floor and two more people squeezed on.

"When are you gonna order me one of those fancy electric wheelies, Doc?" Abercrombie demanded as the doors shut once again.

"When your physical therapist recommends it and I see even a trace of evidence that it's warranted."

They'd ritualistically engaged in this conversation since Abercrombie had come to Shady Lawn for continued physical therapy following his acute hospitalization for a stroke. Despite his surliness, Esa liked Abercrombie's wry sense of humor and sharp wit. He'd quickly become one of Esa's favorite patients. She realized that he grumped constantly to her about the wheelchair because he knew that her consistent reply gave him hope.

"In other words, *never*," Abercrombie grumbled. "Both you and my physical therapist always say I'm too strong for an electric chair."

"You are," Esa replied cheerfully. "Anyone who has the energy for being as ornery as you are doesn't need electricity to power him. If we put you in some pimped-out chair you'll get so lazy and out of shape that blinking will make you out of breath."

"Doc Ormond tells it like it is," Mr. Ostrowski said before he glared at the man and woman who tried to get on the packed elevator when the doors opened on the fourth floor. "Are ya blind as well as brain dead? Wait for the next one!"

Esa sighed. "Thanks, Mr. Ostrowski. Coming from you that's a real compliment."

When they exited the elevator Esa strayed in the direction of the Shady Lawn dining room as she chatted with Mrs. Fuentes. The large room was decorated with black and orange streamers and plastic jack-o-lanterns.

"Hey, Doc."

"Yes, Mr. Abercrombie?" she asked when she saw him waiting alone in the corridor. She walked toward him.

"I watched you park that red car of yours in that postage stamp-sized parking space this morning from my window on the seventh floor this morning. Nine out of ten people wouldn't have attempted the maneuver. Nine out of ten of the ones who tried would have never come close to making it. You drive like you got balls."

"Thanks," Esa said, surprised how pleased the compliment made her feel.

"Must be that fancy new sports car that's put that restless look on your face."

Esa frowned. The man possessed the observatory talents of a spy. "It's my sister's, Mr. Abercrombie. I don't like sports cars."

"Could have fooled me."

His comment reminded her bit too potently of Finn saying something similar while the dawn sunlight turned his sexy, tousled hair into pure gold.

"What's your point, Mr. Abercrombie?"

"I'm going into that dining room right now and eat my low-fat, high-fiber plate o'crapola and unglue my dentures chewing on sugar-free candy because I got nowhere else to go, see? You've got a good head on your shoulders, a healthy young body and a car fast enough to take you to hell and back in ten minutes flat. So my point is, haven't you got any place better to be?"

Esa's mouth fell open.

"No?" Abercrombie answered for her. "Well, take my advice, Doc. *Find* a place."

Esa shifted on her feet indecisively. "Well, I suppose you're right. I still have to pick up Carla at the office and Friday night traffic is going to be a nightmare."

"I'd even choose Dan Ryan traffic over this," he said as he started to wheel his chair into the dining room.

"Mr. Abercrombie?"

He paused and looked over his shoulder. "Yeah?"

"You have someplace else to be. Home. Just give me a little more time. Another two weeks of therapy and you're going to be doing laps around the physical therapy gym with your walker. If you give me three I might even send you home with a cane."

"Yeah?"

"Yeah," Esa replied.

He snorted and resumed rolling down the hallway. But Esa had caught the look of hope that blazed into his blue eyes.

It was enough to make her smile broadly for the first time during the whole work week as she walked out Shady Lawn's front door into the crisp autumn evening.

A half hour later Esa's moment of euphoria had evaporated. She swallowed what felt like gravel in her throat. Not only were they approaching the dreaded 63th Street viaduct in brain-numbing traffic, Carla had just sprung on her where she was going to tonight.

"You mean you're actually going to be at Finn's—I mean Jess'—grandmother's house?"

"I think Jess said that his grandmother lives with his mother."

"She used to be an actress and loves to dress up, so she has this thing for Halloween. She has a big party every year," Esa mused, recalling a few of Finn's warm stories about his Grandma Glory.

"How do you know that?"

Esa shrugged. "Where else? Finn told me."

Carla opened her mouth to question her about that but several cars passing them in the left lane caught her attention. "Jeez, Esa, why do we always have to be in the slow lane? It's going to take forever to get home and—"

"So did Jess tell you it was a costume party?" Esa interrupted, undeterred by Carla's complaints.

"Hmmm? Yeah, but Jess said I didn't have to dress up. All the kids wear costumes but only some of the adults."

"Mind telling me why you're just springing this on me now?" Esa asked. Out of the corner of her eye she saw Carla's offended look.

"Since when do I have go to you for date approval? It's not like *we* had plans tonight. If anyone, Kitten's the one who has a right to be pissed. She gets back from Indianapolis this evening. I was supposed to meet her at Top Choice for a drink."

"I wasn't talking about the actual details of your date," Esa lied as she let up the brake to move forward two inches in traffic. "I was talking about the fact that you and Jess obviously have a thing going on."

Carla snorted. "That should have been obvious to you last weekend, Esa."

Esa studied her best friend with concern. She'd been notably less gung-ho over the flirting in traffic scheme in the past week, but non-forthcoming as to why. Once she'd rallied and stated firmly that she was going to be checking out a pipe-layer at 47th Street.

On the designated evening, Carla had been desperately trying to search the dozens of construction workers once they'd reached the vicinity of 47th Street when Esa realized that several cars around them were honking their horns. She'd glanced up, her eyes widening.

"I think I've found your guy, Carla. It looks like he brought some friends."

"What? Where?" Carla had demanded.

Esa pointed. On top of the viaduct, five men were lined up side by side mooning the swarm of drivers below them. The letters C-A-R-L-A had been emblazoned on their bare butts with red paint.

Carla's pretty face had gone rigid in sheer disbelief. "What in the world are they *doing*?"

"I think it's your guy's idea of flirting. Take it as a compliment." Esa had tilted her head and studied the singular phenomenon. "You know, the letter R isn't bad. Not bad at all."

Carla had stared at her incredulously. They'd both burst out laughing at the same moment. Esa had honked louder than anyone as they'd passed under Carla's tribute.

But Esa didn't think that little episode was the only reason Carla had lost her former enthusiasm for the flirting in traffic idea. She was worried Jess Madigan had something to do with that.

All in all, Esa thought it would be best for both of them to avoid Madigan men altogether.

"I know you had a *thing* with Jess that one night. I just didn't think it had become *more* of a thing," Esa said presently.

Carla waved her hand dismissively. "Don't make too big of a deal of it. I don't."

"Yes, you do," Esa replied, hearing the forced quality of her friend's casual attitude. "Or you want to, anyway. Be careful about him, Carla. Jess Madigan probably has a little black book for every letter of the alphabet."

Carla shot her a fulminating look. "You think I don't know that? I wasn't born yesterday. I haven't heard a peep from him all week. He just called me this afternoon. The date he had lined up probably cancelled at the last moment. Hey, I'm all too willing to stand in for her. Jess is amazing...no, *phenomenal* in bed. I can't believe you didn't sleep with Finn. I'll bet that stuff runs in the family."

"You're sick."

"That's not sick. You know very well what I mean."

Esa stared straight ahead, conscious of Carla studying her and knowing full well what was coming next. She'd heard it six times a day for the past week.

"Why won't you tell me what happened when you and Finn left One Life last week? What could be so terrible? Was his apartment disgusting? Did he have bad breath? Did *you*?"

"Carla, just drop it, okay?" Esa grated out. Without thinking she whipped the little car into the left lane and zoomed forward twenty feet before she slammed on the brakes again. She glanced over at Carla, who studied her with frank suspicion.

"I've never seen you act this way. Do you want to hear what I think, Esa?"

"*No*," she replied pointedly.

"I think that you have a major crush on the hunky Finn. What sane woman could be eaten alive by him like he was doing to you in that hallway at One Life and not be ready to beg him to take up full-time residence in her bed? How could anybody screw up something that looked so fantastic?" Carla demanded. She groaned suddenly when she heard her own question.

"God, Esa. Only you could hose down something that hot."

She didn't know what she thought was worse—her friend's suspiciousness and impertinent questions about Finn or the pitying look Carla was giving her.

"For your information, Finn Madigan was far, *far* from being uninterested," Esa retorted.

"So?" Carla prompted.

"It's...just...he...thinks I'm..."

"*What?*"

"He thinks I'm a casual weekend fling...a-a wild sex kitten."

Carla's blue eyes went wide. "Where would he get that idea about *you*?"

Esa shot her a dirty look.

"Sorry. Of course you're beautiful, Esa—although it would be nice if you at least tried to do something with your hair once in a while. But that's not the point," Carla added quickly when she saw Esa's snarl.

"I don't suppose the fact that you dragged me into that sleazy picking-up-men-on-the-side-of-the-road scheme or that I was driving a car with license plates that read *SXKITN69* could *possibly* relate to Finn thinking I'm a slut, could it?"

Carla just stared for a moment before she started giggling, undeterred by Esa's glare. "Kitten thought something like this might happen."

"I knew it!" Esa fumed. "I *knew* Rachel was behind all of this."

"She didn't know precisely. I mean, how could she? She just wanted you to have a little fun, that's all," Carla explained.

Esa shook her head in disgust. Since they were kids, Rachel had relished poking her fingers into Esa's life and stirring things into a frothy boil.

"Do you really want to know what happened with Finn Madigan?" Esa asked in a burst of fury.

"What?" Carla asked, straightening in the bucket seats.

"Okay, how does this grab you—we were making out in his bedroom and his ex walked in on us."

"Oh my God!" Carla exclaimed, scandalized. "Was it a guy?"

Esa did a double take. "A *guy*? Why would you say that?"

"I don't know," Carla replied, wide-eyed. "You made it sound like it was the most bizarre, humiliating experience ever."

"It was *worse* than a guy. His former live-in and fiancée is *Julia Weatherell*." Esa gave a smug look when Carla gasped loudly.

"Julia Weatherell? That bitch who used to try to blackball Kitten all the time and then hide that trench mouth of hers with all those superior looks, like she was too high and mighty to have even heard those words before let alone have said them?"

"Yep."

"She dropped out of the scene at around the same time you did," Carla mused.

"Must have been during the time period she was involved with Finn," Esa surmised. "You remember how jealous she was about her men. She wouldn't want to go public with a man as gorgeous as Finn Madigan. No, she'd love keeping that secret all to herself. Not that I believe for a second Finn would have gotten into squiring her around to nightclubs and charity events. I get the impression he's a very private person."

"And now she's involved with that rich guy, Graves, and she's popping up on the scene all over again, now as a society *matron* instead of a player," Carla continued. "*Please.* Julia Weatherell is about as matronly as Marie Antoinette. She's about as caring for the poor and downtrodden as old Marie, as well. So…what's Gavin Grave's new girlfriend doing showing up in Finn's bedroom? As if I have to ask."

Esa definitely didn't need to ask. Knowing what she knew about Finn's lovemaking skills and Julia's lack of morals, the fact that Julia was eager to get back in Finn's bed didn't surprise her in the least.

A prickle of panic went through her when she saw how close they'd drawn to the Madigan Construction trailer. She'd changed lanes twice now unconsciously while she had this annoying conversation with Carla.

"He was passed out in their hotel room at the time Julia paid Finn her little visit," Esa explained grimly as she deftly got over in the right lane, earning a scowl from the guy she'd cut off the first time. "Apparently she's miserable and regrets nothing more than leaving Finn. Or the sex, anyway."

"I'll bet," Carla muttered snidely.

"What are you doing?" Esa asked sharply when Carla grabbed her cell phone.

"Calling Rachel. She's going to *die* when she hears about this. You know the hell Julia has put her through in the past. Rachel's always hunting for some dirt on Julia for *Metro Sexy* but that woman cleans up her tracks like a real pro. Until now, anyway."

"Don't you *dare*!" Esa shrieked as she grabbed the phone and hit the disconnect button.

"What's your problem?" Carla asked in open-mouthed disbelief. "Since when do you care about what happens to Julia Weatherell?"

Esa gritted her teeth and stared out the window. They were in the midst of practically standstill traffic and almost directly parallel with the white trailer with the green letters that read Madigan Construction. The fact of the matter was she *couldn't* care less about Julia. But she would do just about anything to make sure Finn's name wasn't dragged through the mud. She felt silly revealing her protective instincts for a weekend fling to Carla, however.

"I told you that in confidence," Esa said.

Carla made a hissing sound of disgust, grabbed her phone from Esa's hand and tossed it into her purse. Esa exhaled with relief. That was the end of that. Carla may annoy the crap out of her at times but she was a true friend. She would never betray a confidence.

"So what are you going to do about all of it?" Carla demanded after pouting for all of three seconds.

"Do?"

"About Finn Madigan?"

Esa directed her gaze to Carla. "I'm not going to *do* anything."

Carla sighed. "I *knew* you had a thing for him. I hate Julia Weatherell. I knew she'd eventually leave scars on one of the Ormond sisters."

"Don't be ridiculous. Finn was a fling, you know that. I hardly had enough opportunity to be *scarred*, either by him or his connection to Julia."

Carla sat up slowly, her face intent as she stared out the window. "A one-night stand, strangers in the night, 'I had a little too much to drink last night, did you notice where I left my panties' kind of thing — is that what you mean?"

"Exactly," Esa replied, confused by Carla's manner.

"Well then you're gonna love this."

"What do you mean?" Esa asked.

Carla nodded pointedly. "Here comes your stranger."

Esa looked in time to see Finn vault over the concrete barrier at the side of the road with athletic ease. He wasn't going to—

He *was*.

She stared in wide-eyed disbelief as he walked straight into four lanes of traffic, his eyes fastened directly on her.

Chapter Eleven
☙

Finn glanced at the now rumpled issue of *Metro Sexy* magazine that lay on his paper-stacked desk. It held no answers for him so he wasn't sure why he kept staring at it.

Work had kept him mind-numbingly busy all week. Now that the air was cooling outside the truth could no longer be denied by Jess or the rest of his crew that winter was coming, making the deadline loom large for their claim on the hefty bonuses Finn had offered for bringing the project in on time. He'd gotten home near midnight every night this week, but they'd managed to finish a long, satisfying stretch of road northbound into the city.

He'd been so busy that he hadn't had much of an opportunity to think about Esa or her second abrupt departure from his condo.

Or maybe he'd kept himself so busy so that he wouldn't take the chance to stew on the matter. The realization that her dramatic exit last Sunday had bugged him even more than Julia's equally dramatic entrance left him unsettled, to say the least.

Despite his weariness, thoughts of Esa would creep into his awareness in the wee hours of the morning. He'd think of that calm yet exultant expression on her beautiful face as she sped down Lake Shore Drive at dawn. It seemed that his body had been programmed to become aroused every time he merely glanced at his whirlpool tub and thought of Esa there, whimpering in pleasure as an orgasm shuddered through her body.

He'd tried to contact her. One time he'd even been desperate enough to call the number for the corporate offices provided in the small print on a glossy page of *Metro Sexy*. But that had been as useless as calling the numbers Caleb had provided him via the Department of Motor Vehicles. A perky receptionist had explained that Kitten Ormond was out of town on business this week, and would he like her voicemail?

Finn had said no. He'd had enough of Esa's seven-word recorded requests to leave a message and she'd get back. She hadn't got back. Not once. He'd left two messages for Esa on Sunday—one on her cell and one on her home phone. Just a half hour ago he'd stifled his pride with extreme effort and made a third call, saying that he'd like to see her tonight so that he could explain face-to-face about what had happened with Julia in his condo.

He doubted anything good could come from chasing after Esa Ormond when she obviously had decided she'd gotten everything from him that she required. Maybe he possessed some kind of inherent deficiency, something that made him lust after women who belonged to organizations like the Junior League or the City Club and considered where you attended school to be more important than what you were made of.

Not that he thought Esa was like Julia. Not *really*. Problem was, his confidence in his ability to judge a person's character had taken a brutal blow after Julia had walked out on him. How could anyone really know another person's true personality until a crisis occurred, something like his father's unexpected death?

Esa confused the hell out of him. He'd read the column she wrote for her magazine. Although he could give a rat's ass about social and celebrity gossip, he had to admit her intelligence and wit came through loud and clear in her writing.

Still, there was something strange about reading her words, as though they didn't quite fit the woman who he'd come to know over the weekend. Close...but not quite, as

Flirting in Traffic

though he tried to focus on Esa through a pair of somebody else's glasses.

He tossed down the magazine in a burst of irritation. Come to think of it, that pretty much described his entire experience with that annoying, prickly...incredibly sexy woman. Maybe part of his attraction was associated with the fact that it was clear as bold print that she was holding back from him. As opposed to his experience with Julia, where he'd thought he'd known her as well as he knew himself.

And in reality knew jack shit.

His head came up when the trailer door swung open.

"Hi," he greeted his sister Mary Kate. "You leaving?"

Mary Kate took off her hardhat, allowing a thick blonde braid to fall down her back. "Yeah, I'm already running late. I promised Grandma Glory I'd be over at the house an hour early to get things ready for the party. Adam said he'd pick up Cory from basketball practice and take all three trick-or-treating while I help out. Little monsters are more excited for the party than they are to be begging for free candy."

Finn grinned as he recalled the manic childhood excitement created by Grandma Glory's annual Halloween Party. Halloween rivaled Christmas in a Madigan child's affections. "I can understand why. We were always the same way."

"Yeah. It was a lot better when *I* was the one getting hepped up on sugar, begging our uncles to play Wolf Man and getting scared witless while we ran around like savages and trampled the neighbors' gardens."

"No doubt," Finn chuckled. His mirth quieted after a moment.

"I guess Mom told you about Grandma Glory's physician's suggestion that they consult a neurologist in regard to these spells Glory has been having?"

Mary Kate looked angry. "Yeah, she told me. That's ludicrous. Grandma Glory is one of the sharpest women I've ever met in my life. She is *not* getting Alzheimer's—or any other kind of dementia. So she's getting a little moody and testy sometimes, so what? Doesn't a woman deserve to get pissy once in a while after she's lived seventy-five years?"

Finn held up his hand in a defensive gesture. "Hey, I'll be the first to agree that I sincerely doubt Glory has dementia. But I saw for myself when one of those spells struck her a few days ago. Mom's right. It *is* concerning. She seems like...I don't know, like she's having a personality change or something. She wasn't just testy, Mary Kate. She was downright *mean*. I'm glad she's going to the neurologist, especially since Glory has pretty hazy recall about the incidents afterward."

"I suppose you're right," Mary Kate said doubtfully.

Finn glanced up expectantly when his sister didn't move after that despite her previous statement that she was running late.

"I'm probably stupid for telling you this but...what the hell."

"What are you talking about?" Finn asked.

Mary Kate shook her head after studying him for a few seconds, a disappointed expression on her pretty face. "Remember earlier this week, how you asked me to keep an eye open for a red Ferrari passing in evening traffic?"

"Yeah," Finn said as he rose from his chair.

"Well, I just saw one about a mile back as I drove to the trailer. It was snagged in that crap out there," she said, nodding her head in the direction of the inevitable Friday evening traffic jam.

"Did you see the license plates?" Finn asked as he came around the desk.

"Yeah. You must be hanging around Jess too much. Since when did you go for the type of woman who would put *SXKITN69* on her license plates?" Mary Kate wondered, clearly disgusted by what she perceived to be her big brother's unusual display of male idiocy.

"Hell if I know," Finn admitted as he moved hastily past Mary Kate toward the door.

Christ, his sister had a right to scold him, Finn thought grimly as he leapt over the concrete barrier a few seconds later. He was acting no better than a beast...a bull charging with single-minded intent at a red-haired woman in a red car.

Amazing what lust could do to a guy.

He glanced briefly at the man driving the dark blue pickup in the first lane, ensuring himself the dude didn't decide he suddenly needed to close the one-foot distance between his truck and the car in front of him until Finn passed. He tapped on the hood of the next car, garnering the attention of a blonde young woman chatting almost nonstop on a cell phone before he passed in front of her. She stopped talking and gaped at him as he walked past.

He didn't know exactly what to expect from Esa at that moment, but he was strangely gratified by the fury that flared in her beautiful eyes as she rolled down her window.

"What the *hell* do you think you're doing walking into the middle of an interstate? You could have just killed yourself!"

His eyes flickered over to Carla, who watched him with avid fascination. He frowned. She suddenly smirked. He looked back at Esa.

"Hello to you too. Traffic is at a standstill. Don't you think you're being a little dramatic?"

"*Hello?*" she raged. "You expect me to exchange pleasantries with you standing in the middle of traffic? Maybe we should talk about the weather while a semi runs over your ass!"

"Esa's always been a worrier," Carla explained pleasantly as she leaned forward. "Did Jess tell you that I was coming to your Grandma's party tonight?"

Finn's eyes flew to Esa's face at the mention of Grandma Glory's party. Had her cheeks just turned pink in embarrassment or had they been that way before?

"I haven't had a chance to talk to him about it. We've been crazy busy at work," Finn said impatiently. "Why haven't you returned my calls?"

He took in her amazed expression. "I don't know what you're talking about."

"It's a simple enough question. Couldn't you have at least done me the courtesy of returning my calls? I wanted to explain...about Julia."

Carla gasped. "Yeah, Esa, couldn't you at *least* have done that?"

"I-I never heard a word from you! And it's none of your business one way or another," she informed Carla sourly.

Finn took one look at Esa's furious, confused expression and knew she was telling the truth. She may not always be honest with her mouth but her face and eyes didn't seem capable of telling a lie.

"I've called you several times this week."

"You may have been calling somebody but it wasn't me," Esa replied defiantly.

Finn considered the terse message on the voicemail that he'd been calling and silently acknowledged that Caleb had possibly gotten the phone numbers incorrect—although it certainly had *sounded* like Esa's voice. Still, the message had never said an actual name.

He didn't have time to belabor the point when the guy in the car behind Esa started honking his horn repeatedly. Finn shot him an irritated, disbelieving look when he noticed the space that had opened up in front of Esa's car, which measured all of ten feet.

"I suppose I could have gotten the wrong number from Caleb."

"Who's Caleb?" Esa asked.

"He's my cousin—a state police officer. It doesn't matter who he is." He leaned down and spoke softly near her ear.

Flirting in Traffic

"The point is that I asked you to come to my grandmother's Halloween party tonight in Bridgeport."

Her eyes got bigger behind her glasses. "Oh. I see."

"Not that I'm forgiving you for taking off like that all of a sudden *again*. Still, I can see how it must have been a little…disconcerting for you."

She snorted at what she must have considered to be a bald understatement.

"Will you come?" he asked, hoping like hell that was excitement making her pulse leap at her throat and not anxiety about being accosted by a madman in the middle of traffic.

The horn behind them blared loudly.

"O-okay," she said unevenly.

He grinned. Even the jerk blasting his horn behind him didn't seem half so annoying. "I'll pick you up then. At eight?" he asked as he stood.

"I-I, uh…I think it'd be best if I met you there."

"I'll come with her," Carla piped up. She leaned over the console to look up at him. "Jess invited me to the party but he said he needed to help your mom and grandma out. I said I'd get there on my own. He gave me the address."

Finn frowned as he transferred his gaze to Esa. She stared up at him, her full, pink lips parted, a bewildered expression on her pretty face. She looked so soft at that moment…so vulnerable.

He resisted an urge to lean down and give her a long, thorough kiss through the car window.

He'd prefer to pick her up himself so that she didn't have such an easy manner of escaping him yet again. But he'd take her any way he could get her.

For the moment, anyway.

"I left you the address on your cell phone, but seeing as how it wasn't the right number… You're sure you have the address?" he asked Carla. She nodded eagerly.

"I'll see you at eight then." He gave Esa a hard look, daring her to call him a liar, before he made the return trip walking through Dan Ryan traffic.

Chapter Twelve

Esa was so nervous by the time she parked the car at 7:58 that evening that she felt like a sixteen-year-old on the night of her junior prom.

"Jeez, Jess wasn't kidding when he said that the party would be packed, was he?" Carla said as they got out of the car and followed a football player and a mummy down the street. Sounds of rock music and children shouting with glee filtered through the pitch-black night. Esa had had to park three blocks away, the streets surrounding Finn's mother's house were so packed with partygoers' cars.

"Finn implied he was related to half of Bridgeport by blood or marriage," Esa recalled.

"Maybe I should have worn a costume," Carla mused, her eyes on the bright white bandages of the mummy walking in front of them. "Something sexy…a French maid's outfit or something."

"That'd have made stellar first impression on Jess' mom."

Carla snorted. "As if it matters what kind of an impression I make on *her*."

Esa was too distracted to respond. Ever since she'd learned from Finn that he'd tried to call her this week she hadn't been able to think about anything properly. She glanced down at her body in the darkness, assuring herself that she hadn't put on her clothes inside out. She recalled Carla's uncustomary warm praise about her hair and outfit earlier when Esa had picked her up, so she supposed she hadn't been so out of it that she'd applied two different colors of eye shadow on each lid or something.

Somewhere in all that mental stewing she'd decided that she'd tell Finn the truth about her. Tonight.

She was sick of lying to him. She hadn't engaged in such a bald-faced lie since her undergraduate days. Even back then her mother had suspected the truth about her moving into her smarmy boyfriend Jarvis' tiny, disgustingly dirty studio.

This was different, of course. Finn wasn't her *mother*. So what if he no longer wanted to *hook up* with her—reprehensible phrase—once he understood she didn't regularly engage in casual sex flings and work as the publisher of a racy singles' magazine? Why would she want to be around him if that were the case, anyway?

So that you can get in a few more rounds of what was most likely the best sex you'll ever have in your life? a sly voice in her head answered.

Well…there was *that*. She wouldn't be a terrible person for wanting good sex. She certainly wouldn't be any more single-minded than Finn himself.

But something strange had occurred when she'd seen Finn walking toward her in traffic with that determined expression on his handsome face. Something that made the blood run so fast in her veins that she'd felt lightheaded. A heretofore unknown feeling had overcome her at the sight of him stalking through those cars like a tawny lion on the hunt. The sensation amplified until she was rendered nearly speechless by the time he'd leaned down and she'd caught his scent.

How was it possible that a man could have such a profound effect on her body? Esa wondered as she and Carla followed the football player and the mummy up the stairs to the crowded front porch. Lit jack-o-lanterns of various sizes with facial expressions that ranged from the eerie to the comical glowed festively along the porch parapet. The rowdy notes of *Ballroom Blitz* sounded through the opened front door.

"Hi Chase...that's not Marisa under all those bandages, is it?" an attractive woman in her fifties with stylishly cut short blonde hair teased.

"Nah, she's coming with her sister Angie in a bit," Chase said as he took off his helmet and gave the woman a hug. "You know Seamus Hatfield right, Mrs. M.?"

The woman's eyes narrowed as she studied Seamus the Mummy. "Used to play football with Finn in high school? Running back, if I recall correctly."

"You've got a good memory, Mrs. Madigan."

She laughed. "You're right. A good memory is a necessity of life with all these kids, grandkids and cousins. Go on out to the deck, you two. The kegs are out there and Danny's got burgers and brats on the grill. There's more food than you'll know what to do with in the kitchen."

"And what about the..." Chase asked as he mimed dealing cards. "I'm planning to win back some of the money that your two oldest sons took from me a couple weeks ago."

"They're playing cards in the family room, not that I'm condoning gambling, mind you."

Chase moved forward and Finn's mother caught sight of Carla and Esa.

"Oh, hello! I'm sorry, I didn't see you behind these two big guys. I'm Molly Madigan."

Chase and Seamus turned to examine them as Esa and Carla introduced themselves and shook hands with Molly.

"Two women that look like them? They gotta be Finn's, Jess', Caleb's...or maybe even Danny's dates. Danny's getting up there...starting to play with the big boys," Chase speculated.

He laughed when Esa glanced at him in surprise, giving away the near accuracy of his guess. He leaned forward and spoke close to Molly Madigan's ear but loud enough for Esa and Carla to hear. "What kind of boys did you raise, Mrs. M., that they don't even go and pick up their dates?"

"Finn offered," Esa said quickly, more to Molly than Chase. She'd already learned from Finn that the neat, attractive woman who stood in front of her wouldn't take kindly to the idea of one of her sons behaving rudely. "I just wanted to drive."

"Oh, so you *are* Finn's friend? He told me to look out for you. And as for Jess, he's been busy helping Glory and me set up for the party," Molly assured Carla, as though she were worried she might have been offended by Chase's teasing. She took Esa by the arm. "Now, come on, you two, and we'll look for them. I hope they're not at cards already…or playing Wolf Man, now that it's dark…"

Carla shot Esa a dubious glance of amusement behind Molly's back but there wasn't much of a chance to either tell their kind hostess that she needn't worry about attending to them personally or ask her what she meant by "playing Wolf Man". The foyer and homey living room that they walked into was so loud with boisterous conversations and rambunctious music that all Esa could do was concentrate on following Molly through the crowd.

"Oh, there's Jess. *Jess!*" Molly called out.

Esa spotted Jess out on the back terrace, leaning back on the railing with a beer bottle in his hand and chatting with another tall young man with sun-burnished light brown hair holding a spatula and dressed like a seventies rock star. Given his obvious chef status, Esa guessed he was Finn's younger brother Danny. He smiled at something Jess said, the quick flash of brilliance reminding her poignantly of Finn.

Molly Madigan had certainly given birth to some awesome-looking males, Esa had to admit.

Jess glanced through the opened patio doors and waved happily when he saw Carla. Esa studied his handsome face as Carla went to join him. She was at least partially mollified that he seemed to be genuinely glad to see her good friend. Carla may pretend like Jess Madigan hadn't gotten beneath her skin but Esa saw the familiar signs that indicated otherwise.

Carla had gone through several bad breakups in the last five years. The scars that she'd received from those love-affairs-gone-awry were part of the reason that she'd acquired this new, callous, single-minded attitude regarding men and sex. But Esa could sense Carla's bravado wearing thin when it came to Jess.

And it worried her.

"One down and one to go," Molly shouted over the notes of *Thriller*. "Maybe Finn is in the kitchen getting something to eat."

Esa just nodded and followed her hostess into a crowded kitchen. The music was muffled somewhat when the heavy oak door swung shut. Almost every occupant of the room was a woman. Molly introduced her to so many people that Esa's head spun, but she took extra interest when she was introduced to "Finn's cousin Dina".

There was nothing suspicious about Finn's teacher in the arts of kissing—in addition to God knew what other erotic activities. The attractive brunette who looked about five years older than Esa was as friendly as everyone else Molly introduced her to, so Esa supposed she could only be thankful to Dina for being such an amazing instructor.

Although she hazarded a guess that Finn possessed an innate talent when it came to the kissing department.

She also took extra interest in meeting Finn's three sisters. Anna Jean and Ellen were the youngest—Esa guessed their ages to be around sixteen or seventeen. The purity of Anna Jean's youthful features made her a perfect Joan of Arc while Ellen's pert pug nose and saucy grin made her ideally suited for her surfer girl costume. The oldest of the three, Mary Kate, a pretty woman with a gorgeous mane of blonde hair, studied Esa with frank interest when Molly introduced them.

"Finn was here just a minute ago. Not sure where he went off to," Mary Kate offered politely.

Esa started in alarm when several ear-piercing shrieks of terror penetrated the kitchen windows. She relaxed a little when the combined screams were followed by children's hysterical laughter. Mary Kate and Molly exchanged a knowing glance.

"Cory and Alex must have talked Finn into playing Wolf Man," Mary Kate said.

"Finn is playing Wolf Man? Let's go!" Ellen told Anna Jean before both girls rushed out of the kitchen.

When Mary Kate saw Esa's confused expression she explained, "You'll think we're barbarians no doubt—my husband did the first time he attended one of Glory's Halloween parties—but the Madigans have a tradition whereby we—"

"Scare our children half to death," a voice behind Esa said.

She spun around to face a tall, incredibly striking woman dressed as Cleopatra. Cleopatra herself would have killed to look as gorgeous as this woman did when she was in her seventies.

"Glory Madigan," the woman said with a smile as she held out her bejeweled hand.

"Esa Ormond," Esa replied as she shook Glory's hand and studied her with open fascination. "That costume is amazing. And you look *fantastic* in it."

"Thanks," Glory said with a cheeky grin. She batted her false eyelashes flirtatiously. "I've been working out regularly at the senior center for the past three months. I've lost twelve pounds, but mostly just turned all the fat to muscle," Glory added as an intimate aside to Esa.

"Low-impact aerobics?" Esa asked.

"In addition to water aerobics on Sundays and meditation on Tuesdays."

"I don't suppose your referring to the new senior center on 95th and Ashland?"

Glory looked surprised. "Yes, the facility is wonderful. I'm surprised you know about it. Do you live in the area?"

"No, I just heard about it through the grapevine," Esa responded in a vague fashion.

"Mom's been bound and determined to get into shape in order to wear that costume," Molly explained with a grin.

"Mom and Grandma Glory made it," Mary Kate added.

"Another Madigan tradition," Molly said with a laugh. "We make Glory a different costume every year."

"I'm going to get you into one next year, Molly," Glory said with a determined frown.

From the doubtful expression on Molly's face, Esa guessed that Molly was nowhere near as fond of dressing up as her mother-in-law was.

"Oh...but we never finished telling Esa about the Wolf Man tradition," Molly said.

"It all started with my husband Sean and his six brothers," Glory began. "I had five children and there were hoards of Madigan cousins. One Halloween Sean bought a Wolf Man mask and whipped the kids into a frenzy by hiding in the backyard and making growling noises—"

"I was one of the kids," Molly piped up. "I was in the seventh grade and invited to the party by my best friend Mary Madigan. When we heard those noises in that pitch-black backyard we were *scared*, I can tell you. But when Dad Madigan came bursting out of the bushes wearing that Wolf Man mask we were petrified. I've never screamed so hard in my life."

Esa laughed when she registered the expression of excitement and incredulous fear that the memory still had the power to bring to Molly's face.

"How many masks have we gone through over the years?" Mary Kate asked before she took a sip of beer.

"At least a dozen," Glory replied.

"It was the best part of Halloween," Mary Kate admitted as mirth gleamed in her blue eyes. "Running around out there in the pitch dark, both wanting to find one of the Uncle Wolves and practically peeing our pants we were so scared he was going to jump out from behind a tree and tickle us until we couldn't breathe."

"Sounds like a blast," Esa agreed, grinning.

"Oh, it was. I was just telling Finn this evening that I kind of wish it was me out there instead of my kids," Mary Kate said wistfully.

They all paused when they heard a wolf howl and more shrieks of terror emanating from the backyard, followed by hysterical shouts and laughter.

"From the caliber of those screams, it's gotta be Finn," Mary Kate said.

"He's the favorite Uncle Wolf," Molly explained to Esa.

"Is he?" Esa asked speculatively.

Mary Kate nodded. "Of course my brothers are only truly 'uncles' to *my* kids but that hoard of cousins out there doesn't know the difference. Even my little sisters think Finn is the best Uncle Wolf."

Esa wondered how much her expression revealed her thoughts when Glory gave her a searching look that reminded her very much of how Finn studied her sometimes.

"Well?" the older woman challenged archly. "Why don't you go and find out for yourself?"

"Maybe I will," Esa said slowly. "Where, precisely, is the Wolf Man's territory?"

Glory's grin itself looked a little wolfish as she replied, "Our backyard and the backyards to each side of us."

"Our neighbors are tolerance personified," Molly added wryly.

"Wish me luck then," Esa said before she turned and left the kitchen, smiling to herself at the sound of Glory's chuckle behind her.

Quite a crowd had gathered on the back terrace. Danny, Jess, Carla, Chase and a brunette woman dressed as a gypsy all glanced over at her when she walked out onto the large deck. Carla gave her a puzzled look but Esa just waved and said hello before she descended the steps into the backyard.

She was a little surprised at how quickly velvety, impenetrable blackness of night surrounded her. Finn's mother and grandmother lived in an older, established neighborhood that boasted enormous backyards that ended in an alley. Across the alley, another backyard stretched to the house on the next street. Detached coach-style garages blocked much of the light that shone from the house. The children certainly had an atmospheric arena in which to scare themselves silly.

Esa peered through the darkness, afraid she would trip over a bush or a small child. The night was chilly but not overly so and she wore only a lightweight leather jacket. She paused when she heard the sound of muffled laughter in the distance and little feet scurrying through the leaves.

She suppressed her own nervous giggle of excitement. Why did humans love to scare themselves so much? Something brushed against her outstretched hand and she jumped in alarm, sighing when she realized it was just the bark of a thick tree trunk. Thankfully she hadn't walked straight into it and knocked herself out.

She suddenly went very still when she heard footsteps in the leaves just feet away from her.

"Wolf Man's right on the other side of that tree," Esa barely made out a boy whispering.

"He is not. Quit trying to scare me, Cory," a younger girl's voice responded shakily.

"He *is*. Let's get him before he gets us!"

The sound of rapidly rushing feet made Esa's eyes go wide in panic. "No, wait. I'm not the Wolf Man, I'm Esa...oh—"

She stopped speaking abruptly when the weight of a small body collided against her legs and arms wrapped around her thighs. She teetered for a second, almost losing her balance, but then righted herself and steadied the small body that had attempted to tackle her as well.

"It's a lady," the little girl who had been correct to doubt the presence of the Wolf Man exclaimed.

"Shhh, *quiet,* Amanda. He'll hear you. You'd better not get us caught," a boy admonished.

"Are you all right?" Esa asked as she extricated Amanda from her legs. She bent down and peered at the vague outline in the blackness. From the size of her Esa guessed that she must have been around six or seven years old. She was accompanied by three other children, all of them older, given the sizes of their shadows.

"Are you looking for the Wolf Man too?" the little girl asked in a stage whisper.

"Er...yes, I am."

The girl giggled.

"Let's go, Amanda," one of the boys hissed in a long-suffering big brother voice. They melted back into the darkness and were gone as quickly as they'd come. Esa tried to calm her rapid breathing in the silence that followed.

She left the relatively secure landmark of the tree and wandered to the left of the yard, her arms stretched out in front of her. The children likely knew the territory of the backyards intimately but Esa was not only nearly blind but ignorant as she stumbled around back there. Her fingers encountered a waist-high bush. She tried to move around it but quickly realized it was a hedge that probably separated the two yards.

A light rustling sound reached her hyper-alert ears and she paused. She drew her breath in cautiously but all was silent except for the muted voices and music of the party in the distance. It probably had just been some leaves scattering in the wind. Still, some instinct told her it was more than that.

"Finn?" she queried softly, her heart hammering in her ears. "Is that you?"

When she got no answer she resumed picking her way along the hedge, looking for an opening between the yards. Just when she found a gap in the bushes someone grabbed her from behind...someone who was most definitely *not* a child.

Despite the fact that she'd come there specifically to find him, her nerves got the better of her. A scream rose in her throat. His hand was over her mouth in a second, stifling it.

"What are you afraid of, little girl? Didn't you come looking for a wolf?" he growled near her ear. His voice was muffled by the mask he must be wearing. He sounded both familiar and sinister at once. Esa shivered uncontrollably in fear and something else, something much more powerful.

She twisted her head away from his hand on her mouth, freeing it. She squirmed in his hold. He wrapped her securely in his strong arms, making a mockery of her struggle. His body felt long and hard pressed so tightly against her. Excitement jolted through her with the strength of an electric shock, adrenaline pumping into her veins and a powerful sexual awareness enlivening her flesh.

"Is this how you greet all your dates?" she muttered sarcastically between ragged pants. She yelped in surprise when he suddenly shifted his weight and fell to the ground, bringing her down on top of him. He rolled over until she was lying on her back in the cool grass, his body covering her.

"Only the ones who come looking for it," he said quietly near her face, amusement lacing his tone.

It had all happened so quickly that Esa was momentarily stunned into silence. He must have removed his mask because his voice had sounded normal just now — that low, seductive rumble that she associated exclusively with Finn. His fragrant breath struck her lips and cheeks in choppy bursts of air. His scent reached her nostrils — subtle, spicy aftershave, clean male skin and fragrant leaves. She smiled to herself, realizing she wasn't the first person he'd tumbled in the leaves and grass tonight.

Her fingers came up to touch what she couldn't see, lacing through the thick hair the collar of his jacket. She pressed her fingertips to his skull, applying a downward pressure.

"I guess I was...looking for it, I mean," she whispered breathlessly. "Come here, Wolf Man."

But she needn't have said it because he'd already been on his way.

Despite his aggressive play his lips were gentle and persuasive when they touched hers. Not that Esa required persuading. She curled her fingers in his hair and craned her neck up for more of the taste of him.

"Shhh," he whispered so softly that she barely heard him over the sound of her heart pounding in her ears. He proceeded to nibble and eat at her mouth like it was a rare Godiva truffle that he'd found in the midst of his dime store Halloween candy. Esa felt herself turning to warm, sweet syrup under the influence of that kiss.

She whimpered into his mouth when his tongue slid along her lower lip, politely asking for entrance. Esa granted it, melting into the cool grass beneath the divine heat of Finn's hard body and his intoxicating kiss. When she began to rub her tongue next to his, matching his slow, erotic rhythm, he growled and rocked his erection against her harboring heat. Esa shifted her hips up against him, the resulting friction making their kiss hungrier. She applied suction, pulling him further into her.

"Be careful about teasing, Esa," Finn mock-threatened quietly next to her damp lips a few seconds later. His hand spread along her waist and found its way beneath her jacket, rising slowly up the side of her torso. She shivered almost uncontrollably beneath him despite the fact that heat emanated from his body. "It's a full moon, you know...and you test the beast sorely."

Esa tried to snort in amusement when he flexed his hips for emphasis but was quickly silenced when he slid his hand over her sweater-covered breast. He cupped her softly then shaped her firmly to his palm. Her nipple stiffened against the pressure, sending a sympathetic jolt of pure desire between her thighs. She groaned and rubbed up against him to alleviate the sharp ache.

"*Esa*," he muttered as he continued to mold her breast with his hand and their flesh strained against one another's with growing need. Esa was gratified to hear that all amusement had vanished from his tone.

She heard a child's muffled laughter nearby.

"Finn, *stop*," she whispered. "The kids are—"

"They can't see anything," Finn growled into her neck between hungry kisses.

"Yes, but—"

"I'm just...kissing you... What's the big...deal?" he asked between nibbles of flesh.

The big deal was that Esa was so aroused as she lay there beneath Finn in the middle of his mother's leaf-strewn backyard that it certainly didn't feel like *just kissing* in the slightest.

"But I think they might be—"

"*Now*," someone yelled.

"Right *there*," Esa finished.

"Gotcha, Wolf Man!" a boy yelled at the same time that the weight of several bodies fell on top of them.

"Ow! Hey… Watch the kidneys," Finn ordered between grunts as child after child piled on top of them. Esa broke out in laughter when he covered her body from the tackling kids.

"Tickle him like he does us!"

Esa ducked her head into Finn's chest for protection against the ensuing mêlée of laughing, squirming, tickling children. Finn finally managed to get them off them with a combination of half-serious threats, gentle wrestling and returned tickles.

"There's a lady here. Now cut it out," Finn finally said as he wrestled one of his older, more boisterous nephews while trying to stop two giggling nieces from tickling his ribs. "Go and hide again. You guys conquered this Wolf Man. Another uncle is going to come get you."

"Who, Uncle Finn?" the boy who wrestled with him demanded.

"I don't know, but I'm gonna tell him to hunt you down first if you don't get out of here, Aidan. Hurry up. He'll be out here in a minute."

"Are you okay?" Finn asked softly as the sound of the children's voices faded.

"Yes," Esa said with a laugh as she sat up. "Except for the leaves in my hair."

His hand spread along her neck, his fingers reaching to tangle in her hair. "I'm used to leaves in your hair. It's one of the things I like about you."

Esa froze. Something about the warmth in his tone had taken her by surprise.

It had taken her by *pleasant* surprise. So pleasant that Esa had been caught with her guard down. First there had been a burning-hot desire followed by the playful antics of the children. To have such lighthearted pleasure and fun followed by that indefinable something in Finn's voice just now…the indication that he liked more than *one thing* about her left Esa mentally spinning.

She wondered if he sensed the tension as well when he suddenly removed his hand and stood. He reached for her hand and pulled her up.

"How about we get some food after all that wrestling?"

"Wrestling, huh? Is that what they call it these days?" she asked, joining in his obvious effort to lighten the moment.

His deep laughter made her smile into the darkness. She couldn't decide as they walked through the yard whether or not she was relieved or disappointed to be back in familiar territory with Finn.

Chapter Thirteen

Esa had a good time over the next hour eating her supper in the crowded kitchen at a huge lovingly restored antique oak table with two long benches on each side of it. Finn, Dina, Glory, Ellen, Mary Kate, Danny and Finn's garrulous, good-looking cousin Caleb Madigan all sat at the table, along with two of Danny's friends from graduate school. Apparently Finn's youngest brother Micah had been detained at school by a midterm on Monday morning.

Everyone had already eaten besides Finn, Mary Kate and Esa, but they all talked so much that Esa didn't feel self-conscious about stuffing her face with a cheese veggie burger and delicious homemade potato salad.

She was a little envious of Finn for belonging to such a large, warm, easygoing family. Rachel and she had always been very close with their parents, but four hardly compared to the double- or even triple-digit total number of Finn's close-knit extended family.

She'd discovered during their meal that Caleb was the oldest son of Finn's Uncle Joe. Joe and Ed, Finn's father, had been exceptionally close and owned Madigan Construction together. The two families were closely tied as a result. The fact that the two brothers had died within months of each other pulled those familial bonds even tighter. Caleb looked more like a brother to Finn than a cousin, with burnished brown hair like Danny's and green eyes like Jess'. Unlike Finn or his brothers however, Caleb wore a sexy, neatly trimmed goatee.

Despite all the possible distractions of the loud, friendly banter, the good food and Finn's gorgeous cousin and too-cute little brother, Esa's attention was captured almost completely by Finn, who sat next to her on the wood bench. She was hyperaware of his body next to her, of every casual brush of their arms, of the pressure of his hip against her own.

Once she glanced up to find him watching her with those incredibly blue eyes. What she saw in their depths made her stop chewing. She resumed a second later when she felt him place his hand on her thigh under the table and pull it next to his own hard length but she found it extremely difficult to swallow.

He wanted to make love to her again tonight. That was what she'd read as clearly as a neon sign in his eyes. And Esa knew that was what she wanted too…more than anything.

There was something else Esa knew for a fact in that moment. She was putting much, much more than her self-respect at risk by carrying on this way with Finn. Every minute that she remained with him would just amplify her pain when he eventually stopped wanting to see her. That moment might come as early as tomorrow morning or next month but it would inevitably come. He'd been engaged to be married just a month ago. Rebound relationships never worked out, at least in Esa's experience.

"Hey, I hope there's no hard feelings about giving Finn your phone number, Esa." Caleb interrupted her tumultuous thoughts as Mary Kate and Danny served everyone pumpkin cake and cinnamon ice cream for dessert.

"You *should* apologize," Finn interrupted before Esa could respond. "You gave me the wrong numbers, Sherlock. So much for the dependability of the state of Illinois' law enforcement."

Caleb looked surprised. "Couldn't have."

Finn just gave him a wry glance before he ate a bite of cake.

"I think that Caleb was referring to the infringement on my privacy for non-police business," Esa explained patiently.

Finn didn't bother to respond to the obvious however, and just continued to eat his cake.

"You don't live at 989 North Michigan Avenue?" Caleb persisted.

Esa paused in the process of spooning some ice cream. "So that's how you found me," she said softly to Finn. He smiled as he chewed his cake and gave her thigh a tight squeeze.

"See. I gave you the right information," Caleb said, obviously feeling vindicated by the information. "How could I have gotten the address right and got the phone number wrong?"

Finn's smile faded. He didn't say anything in front of everyone, thank God, but she had the sneaking suspicion that he was wondering if she'd been lying about not receiving those phone calls. It suddenly struck Esa full force that Finn had been calling her evasive, manipulative little sister all week.

"Maybe my DMV information needs to be updated," Esa answered Caleb evasively although her gaze remained on Finn.

No wonder he'd been so confused. She and Rachel sounded very similar and Rachel's messages were always brief and to the point. But why hadn't Rachel bothered to return his calls to alert him of his mistake? More importantly, why hadn't Rachel told Esa about the misunderstanding?

Although that would have required that her sister had returned her calls at least once this week.

What was Rachel up to?

Esa shook her head in frustration and met Finn's doubtful stare.

"I never received any phone calls from you," she assured him. When he resumed chewing again slowly, his eyes still on her, she continued softly enough for only him to hear. "There's been a misunderstanding. I'll try to explain later."

Flirting in Traffic

He merely nodded once.

Caleb looked excited when Esa told him she liked to play poker and was in the midst of asking people at the table who wanted to get a game going when a spine-chilling scream of terror reached all of their ears.

And this scream *hadn't* been a child's.

Her eyes widened in disbelief when the woman followed the eerie shriek by shouting a name.

"*Eeesaaa!*"

Esa flew out the front door directly after Finn. The once-crowded front porch was now empty. She tried to keep up with Finn's long legs as he ran around the side of his mother's house in the direction from which they'd heard the scream.

"What the hell...*Jess?*" Esa heard Finn ask a few seconds later when he came to an abrupt halt in the side yard. She tried to peer around his tall form but she couldn't make out anything in the darkness.

"Get the hell off me, you animal!" a familiar voice shouted from the ground, followed by a man's grunt of mixed surprise and pain.

"*Rachel*? Is that you?" Esa cried out.

"Esa? What kind of a party are you attending anyway? I heard the music and was going around to the back to find you and this...criminal, barbarian...*asshole* attacked me."

"Give me a break. I thought you were one of the kids. You're small enough to be one of the teenagers," Jess said in a mellow tone that surprised Esa, given the bizarre circumstances.

"And that makes it all right, I suppose—attacking a child! Esa, call the police," Rachel ordered.

The panic she heard in her sister's tone took Esa by surprise. She was vaguely aware that several people had come up behind her and were listening to the entire conversation.

"Rachel, he's not a criminal. He was playing Wolf Man. It's a game the Madigans play on Halloween—"

"He knocked me to the ground and then he...he..." Rachel made a strange choking sound of mixed disbelief and outrage. Esa was suddenly very curious as to what exactly Jess Madigan *had* done to her little sister in the dark. "Let me up, you jerk," Rachel screeched.

"I think you need to calm down a little bit before I let you go. You almost gave me a black eye just now with that elbow," Jess replied evenly.

"You bastard," Esa heard Rachel hiss at him, her insult striking Esa as entirely too personal given the circumstances.

Esa opened her mouth to speak when someone stepped up beside her. "Who is that obnoxious person maligning my grandson?"

Esa blinked in surprise at the sheer outrage in Glory Madigan's trembling voice. *Great*. This just kept getting better and better.

"It's okay, Grandma Glory. This is just a misunderstanding," Finn said. But instead of being placated by his reassuring tone, Glory stepped forward aggressively.

"Get off this property, you little strumpet, before I call the police and have you thrown in jail where you—"

"Grandma Glory, calm down," Finn interrupted.

"I'm not calming down when that woman is attacking my grandson!"

Everyone began to talk at once

"Esa, get this idiot off me!"

"Jeez, what are you *doing* here?" Carla suddenly asked from the darkness on the other side of Jess and Rachel.

"Calling the police..." Glory said in a shaking voice that alarmed Esa.

"I *am* the police, Grandma. Finn? What's going on?" Caleb demanded.

"*Quiet* everyone," Esa shouted. She inhaled slowly, gathering her frayed nerves in the silence that followed.

"Rachel, stop acting like a loon and promise not to hit Jess again if he lets you up. I swear—I don't know what's gotten into you. Finn, if you would be so kind as to go to the kitchen and get some orange or apple juice?"

"*What?*" Finn asked incredulously.

"Glory…I apologize for my sister's dramatics." Esa placed her hand gently on the older woman's arm and felt the clamminess of her skin as well as the fine tremor in her flesh. "Why don't we go inside and I'll try to explain."

"Esa?" Rachel asked from the ground in a beleaguered tone.

"Just do as I say," Esa barked before she took Glory's arm and led her through the small crowd toward the house.

She was glad that Glory didn't put up any resistance when Esa guided her down the corridor to the right of the living room.

"Her room is right in here," Molly Madigan directed from behind Esa.

Esa glanced around, thankful for Finn's mother's presence. She led a dazed Glory into her bedroom and set her on the edge of her bed.

"May I see her medications please?" Esa asked Molly briskly as she checked Glory's pulse.

"That woman was your sister?" Glory asked.

"Yes, she's my sister. From the sound of her voice, Jess scared the hell out of her. I've never heard her act that way before," Esa mused as she removed Glory's black Cleopatra wig and unclasped the heavy gold necklace from around her perspiring neck.

"Thank you. I'm so hot…but I can't stop shaking," Glory muttered.

Esa read each of the four pill bottles that Molly had brought her. "Do you have an Accu-Chek, Glory?"

"I'll get it," Molly answered for her mother-in-law.

"Oh, good," Esa said both to Molly and to Finn, who had just entered the room carrying some apple juice. "Set it down there, would you, Finn? When's the last time you ate, Glory?"

Glory's forehead wrinkled as she tried to recall.

"Can't remember," she finally answered dully. "Maybe four or five this afternoon. Didn't want to eat too late and be bursting out of my Cleopatra costume."

Finn's handsome face was creased in mixed concern and confusion when Esa requested that he go and get some food from the kitchen but he went without comment. Esa took the blood glucose monitor from Molly when she returned to the room.

"Is high blood sugar what all of these episodes have been about?" Molly asked.

"This has happened before?" Esa asked sharply.

Molly nodded. "Several times in the past month. Her doctor ran some tests but everything was fine. Glory's been taking diabetes medication for two years now and there's never been a problem. Her sugars weren't that high to begin with and her doctor said that they were well-controlled with the medication," Molly fretted as Esa poked Glory's fingertip with the lancet.

"Ouch!" Glory protested sluggishly.

"A little too well-controlled, I'm betting," Esa said. She nodded her head in self-confirmation when she saw the numbers that came up on the screen and handed Glory the apple juice. "Drink up. Your sugars are low."

"*Low?*" Glory frowned. "I thought I was supposed to be taking medication for *high* blood sugar."

Esa prodded the bottom of the glass as a reminder for the older woman to drink. "You are. But all that exercise and meditation at the senior center is changing the chemical scenery of your body. Your dosage on the diabetic medication is too high. Lots of people have to be recalibrated, so to speak, when they start a regular exercise or meditation routine. I'll bet your blood pressure has gone down nicely as well."

"It has," Molly confirmed. "Her doctor made a point of telling me when we went last week. I made a special appointment because of these periods of irritability. It's out of character for Glory."

"Did you tell your doctor that you've been exercising regularly?" Esa asked Glory when she finished her juice.

"I think so," Glory replied.

"I made a point of telling him if Glory didn't," Molly said.

Esa frowned and took the glass from the now exhausted-looking older woman. If it was true that Glory had lost twelve pounds like she'd reported so proudly to Esa earlier tonight, then her doctor should have questioned her extensively about it as well as her exercise routine and then reevaluated Glory's medication requirements.

Too many physicians—especially the younger ones—were prejudiced when it came to matters of older adults, automatically assuming that any exercise or activity that a woman Glory's age undertook would be minimal and, while beneficial to health, nowhere near the strenuous health club routines they considered to be "real" workouts. But one only had to glance at Glory to know that she was a strong, athletically inclined woman who would do everything she undertook with passion and dedication. Undoubtedly Finn's grandmother could leave Esa in a panting, quivering heap as she ran laps around her at the gym.

It irritated the heck out of Esa knowing how many of her colleagues refused to either recommend meditation to their patients or take into account the sometimes significant effect regular practice had on blood pressure and overall health. The results weren't the same for everyone, of course, but regular meditation had a profound effect on some patients.

Esa refrained from spewing out her anger at incompetent doctors and focused on being productive, however.

"My advice is that you make an appointment first thing in the morning with your doctor," Esa said as she set the Accu-Chek monitor down on the bedside table. "Your medication dosage needs to be looked at in light of your regular exercise and weight loss. What you've just experienced is the irritability, cold sweats and lethargy that comes from extremely low blood sugar. If you like, I can make a recommendation for an excellent physician in your area who specializes in treating older adults. In the meantime, Glory, five small meals per day — and *no* skipping meals to look good in an outfit."

"Finn told us that you were in publishing," Molly said bemusedly.

"Finn's a fool then," Glory mumbled groggily. "She's obviously a nurse or a doctor. I'll wager a doctor from that high-and-mighty tone. How Finn could have brains enough to earn a master's degree both in engineering and architecture and not know what the woman he's seeing does for a living is beyond me."

Esa started in surprise.

"Oh, good," Molly said when Finn walked into the room holding a paper plate. Mary Kate followed, an anxious look on her face. "Give that to Glory, Finn. Her blood sugar is low."

"All four of you aren't going to stand there and stare at me while I eat, are you? Go on and enjoy the party. I'm pooped, I'm going to bed after I finish this," Glory said through a mouth full of bratwurst and bun a moment later.

Molly waved them out of the room. "Go on, you three. I'll stay and help her get out of her costume. And thank you, Esa."

"I'll leave you a note with the name of that physician recommendation, if you'd like it," Esa said softly.

"I would…very much. Thanks again," Molly added, a warm, genuine look of gratitude shining from her green eyes before she closed the door after them.

Chapter Fourteen

Finn leaned against the counter in the kitchen and watched through narrowed eyelids as Esa conferred privately with Rachel in the corner, their communication too soft to be overheard but emphasized by hisses, frowns and sparking brown eyes. The only words he'd been able to make out so far had been uttered by Rachel and had completely confused him instead of throwing any light on the strangeness of the evening.

He's *the one who called* me. *Why shouldn't I be able to at least ask him about such a juicy tidbit? If neither of you will tell me, who will?*

Esa had responded with so much passion that her hair bounced around her shoulders as she energetically shook her head and whispered heatedly. After a moment of bearing her sister's wrath, Rachel appeared to tune her out using some trait universally acquired by younger siblings. Esa ranted while Rachel leaned back and studied Finn with frank curiosity. When he shifted uncomfortably under her gaze she suddenly gave him a bright, warm smile.

He'd immediately known that the stranger in the kitchen was Esa's sister because of her mane of auburn hair. It fell midway down Rachel's back in soft waves that framed a heart-shaped face but it was the precise color of Esa's. Rachel was several inches shorter than her sister and more delicate in overall appearance.

The acid glance of pure distaste that Rachel threw his brother Jess when he walked through the kitchen door with Carla behind was hardly demure, however.

Jess leaned on the counter next to him. Carla rushed across the large room to the corner and joined the symphony of feminine hisses.

"Grandma Glory okay?" Jess murmured.

"She's fine now. Her blood sugar was low. Esa thought to check it with the blood glucose monitor."

Jess grunted distractedly as his gaze returned to the huddle of women. Esa glanced around furtively at Finn and then turned quickly to retort to something Rachel had just whispered.

"Maybe we should go out on the terrace. I feel like I'm watching some kind of secret female ritual."

"No way," Finn replied grimly. "I'd do just about anything to figure out Esa at this point, even if that means spying on a family squabble."

Jess snorted in a mixture of amusement and pity. "You're a goner."

Rachel must have heard Jess speak because she glanced over, curled her lip in scorn and ran her velvety eyes over him scathingly.

"She's a firecracker, isn't she?" Jess mumbled, referring to Rachel.

Finn blinked when he heard the undisguised heat in his brother's voice.

"Must run in the family," Finn mused as he studied Jess speculatively.

Rachel backed out of the huddle and spoke audibly. "All right, fine. Just stop lecturing me about it. We'll talk about it more tomorrow. I'll meet you at Mom and Dad's to trade them. I'm getting out of here. I hope I don't get attacked again on the way back out to the car," Rachel said sarcastically as she walked toward the door.

"I said I was sorry," Jess called out. Rachel refused to even look at him as she stormed out the door.

"She's a little high-strung, your sister," Jess murmured as Carla and Esa approached. Carla looped her arm around Jess' waist and leaned her head against his shoulder.

"Let's go. I'm tired. Jess is going to take me home, aren't you?" Carla asked as she glanced up at Jess seductively.

"Sure," Jess agreed, prying his eyes from the door that still swung back and forth from Rachel's dramatic exit.

Finn waited silently once they'd said their goodbyes to Jess and Carla. He saw the moment when Esa's thoughtful, tense expression altered. She furtively looked around the kitchen and back at him.

"That's right. We're alone," he challenged softly.

She laughed shakily. "The party really cleared out quickly."

"It's amazing how a woman screaming her head off that she's been attacked and the subsequent illness of the hostess can do that to a party."

Esa's face fell. "Oh—I'm so sorry about Rachel. It must seem really strange to you that she came here but...she just... Well, to be honest, I've never seen her act like that. Rachel's usually the cool one. I didn't think she had a hysterical bone in her body."

"And?" Finn prodded. From the pink stain that colored Esa's cheeks he guessed that she was probably dodging the truth again. Anger rose in his chest at the clear evidence of her dishonesty. He tamped it down in self-irritation. Why did he keep expecting her to be something more than she was? He was seeing her in order to have a good time—get back on his feet after few harsh blows in his personal life.

He listened to her blather on.

"And...and...Rachel came because she wanted to switch cars with me," Esa finally concluded.

Finn crossed his arms above his waist. "Switch cars?"

"Yes," Esa assured him brightly. "So, do you want to—"

"And what about all that stuff with Grandma Glory?" he interrupted.

"Oh, *that*?" Esa asked as she pointed in the general vicinity of Glory's bedroom and laughed too loud. She examined him nervously through lowered eyelids. "I can explain about that. See, I've known quite a few people who have had a condition similar to your grandmother's. Funny it came up because I was going to tell you all about it tonight."

"Really."

She looked stung by his sarcasm. He ground his back teeth together when he saw anger flash into her brandy-colored eyes. "Yes, I was. What are you acting so pissy for?"

He uncrossed his arms and straightened. "You know what? I have no idea. You don't owe me anything, Esa."

"Nothing but a good time in bed for a few nights, is that it?" Esa flared.

He met her glare with equal irritation for about ten seconds before he finally exhaled slowly. Why *was* he so fired up? It wasn't Esa's fault that her sister was a hysterical party crasher. And even though he was mystified as hell by the appearance of that calm, authoritative, entirely confident persona that Esa had taken on during the whole incident with his grandmother, he had to admit that it only made her exponentially more appealing to him.

Maybe *that* was at the core of his anger. Esa was really getting to him, rebound fling or not. If he didn't watch himself with her he was going to be the *goner* that Jess had already accused him of being.

He'd been stewing for the last twenty minutes over the fact that he hadn't thought to question Esa's knowledge or motives *once* during the entire incident with Grandma Glory. He might have thought the whole situation was unusual but his confidence in Esa had been complete.

Besides, that smooth, authoritative woman had disappeared and the prickly, insecure, hissing creature was back. He exhaled his irrational irritation and reached out to sooth the hackles he'd raised on Esa. She hesitated for a second when he pulled her toward him but then sank her head and pressed it into his chest.

"I'm really sorry," she muttered against his shirt.

He placed his chin on the top of her head and inhaled the scent of her fragrant shampoo. "No. *I'm* sorry. I should be thanking you for helping out with Grandma Glory that way instead of provoking you. You handled that situation like a pro. Did you use to work as a nurse or something?"

"Er, something like that," she said almost unintelligibly into his chest. He prodded her shoulder and she looked up at him. "It was really nothing though. You just have to be familiar with the signs—"

"It *was* something. Thanks."

His gaze narrowed on her parted lips. She had the prettiest, most kissable mouth he'd ever seen in his life—full, pink lips that always were begging to be sampled…to be penetrated. Just thinking about the honeyed cavern inside made his cock thicken with a stab of undiluted lust. The potent memory of her kneeling between his thighs, using that mouth for the sweetest of sins, flashed graphically into his brain

The arousal that suddenly coursed through his veins felt shockingly strong and imperative. It amazed him to realize that he honestly didn't know if he could wait for the length of time it took to get back into the city in order to have her. She *had* said something about a few nights in bed, hadn't she? A few could technically be…what? Six? Seven? A dozen?

Maybe he could bargain for an extension at the end of his term?

"Let's go to my place," he suggested gruffly.

"Oh…all right."

He grabbed her hand and pulled her hastily toward the door.

* * * * *

Twenty minutes later Esa unlocked the door of Rachel's car so that Finn could squeeze his long frame into the passenger seat. Esa had been puzzled by his terse explanation that they would take separate vehicles from his mother's house. Before they'd separated he'd told her to follow him to the restricted construction area off the 59th Street overpass on the Dan Ryan.

"I've got a surprise for you," he had told her before he'd ducked his head and kissed her through the car window, quick and potent, and then left to get in his own vehicle.

"Why are you leaving your truck here?" Esa asked, eyeing the white pickup truck where he'd parked it next to a bulldozer that read Madigan Construction on the side of it.

"I don't need it. I've got my car at home and I can always take the 'L' to get to work. I usually only use the truck to get back and forth along the highway during work hours."

Esa couldn't help but feel like an insider as she gazed at the huge machinery and the brand-new stretch of pristine white road that led just inside the barricade. On the other side of the cement barricade traffic moved at a sluggish thirty miles per hour even at eleven-fifteen at night.

Finn readjusted the seat so that it went back as far as possible.

"When I was with your Grandma Glory earlier she said that you have master's degrees both in architecture and engineering," Esa stated baldly.

He paused for a fraction of a second in the process of pulling on his seat belt.

"Yeah. Is the number of degrees I have important to you or something?" he asked with a stiff jaw as he fastened his seat belt.

"Yes...I mean *no*, not in some kind of nasty way. I'm not...you know, hanging around you for your *diplomas*," she replied with a roll of her eyes. "It just struck me when she said it because you'd never told me. Jeez, Julia really did a number on you, didn't she?" Esa mumbled under her breath after a strained silence.

He shifted in his seat, seeming entirely too big for the confines of the sleek sports car. "I've wanted to talk to you about Julia. I'm sorry about what happened last weekend. I was as shocked about Julia showing up as you were."

"I know. I mean, it seemed pretty obvious that you were surprised. Besides, you don't owe me any explanations," Esa added with a sinking feeling, thinking about Finn saying something similar earlier.

She felt his gaze on her. "I do. For the discomfort you experienced—I at least owe you something for that."

Despite the anxiety the topic of Julia provoked, Esa's lips twitched slightly. Molly Madigan would approve of her son's manners.

"So...Julia Weatherell was the fiancée they you told me about. The one who walked out when you decided to take over your dad's business?" Esa prompted.

He nodded. She listened while Finn explained in more detail about his father and uncle dying and leaving a faltering business, his decision to sell the architecture and design firm that he'd developed with a friend, the resulting fights between Julia and him and her ultimate decision to leave.

"She was dead set against me selling my shares in the firm to Jason. When she realized I wasn't going to change my mind about getting Dad's business on solid ground again she decided to leave. I guess she felt like I was saying my family was more important than she was."

"If that's the way she felt, she was being unfair. You weren't choosing your family over her. It didn't have anything to do with *her*," Esa said sourly. Although of course Julia would have made it all about *her*—her needs, her expectations, her image. Never mind the fact that her fiancé was suffering from the abrupt death of his father and that his family required support. Never mind that *Finn* had needed someone in his corner.

Hearing about Julia's selfishness always irritated her but hearing about what she'd done to Finn got her really boiling.

He shrugged. "She's got a high-profile job. Apparently having a partner who fits her image is more important to her than I'd ever imagined. That's how it is sometimes. You never really know what a person is really made of until the bombs fly."

Esa scowled in the semi-darkness.

"But Julia hasn't given up the hope of being with you, despite the fact that she doesn't want to marry a guy who works in construction. Am I right?"

"I can't control what Julia does or thinks, Esa."

"No, I don't suppose you can," Esa conceded.

That still didn't answer all her unasked questions about how he really felt about Julia, her betrayal...or relationships in general for that matter. But did she really need to ask? It seemed pretty obvious Finn was still nursing some pretty raw wounds—certainly significant enough injuries to keep him well out of the dating arena.

They sat for a moment in thoughtful silence.

"Traffic's still pretty bad, huh?" he observed, an obvious attempt at breaking the weighty silence.

Esa exhaled tiredly as she shifted the car into drive. Even the word "traffic" seemed to drain her of energy nowadays.

"Uh uh," Finn said sharply when she started to take the restricted ramp back onto the overpass so that they could merge onto the Dan Ryan. "Keep going on this road."

Esa stared at him wide-eyed. "But it's not even finished yet, is it?"

Finn's eyes gleamed in the semi-darkness. "As of yesterday, one driving lane as well as the emergency lane are finished and cleared. We'll open up the extra express lane come Monday but tonight...it's wide open."

Esa braked, bringing the car to an abrupt stop.

"You mean this road is clear sailing all the way into the city?" Esa asked, excitement making her voice tremble slightly.

"That's my surprise to you."

Esa just stared at him for a few seconds. Suddenly she laughed and pressed her foot to the accelerator.

The thought struck her as they blew past the cars moving sluggishly in traffic to the right of them that Finn had just given her a gift. And even though she hadn't known him for that long, it was the most intimate, exhilarating...*wonderful* gift she'd ever been given.

"I felt like I was *flying*," Esa exclaimed ten minutes later as she came to a neat stop inside of Finn's parking garage.

"That's because we were."

For the first time Esa realized he looked a little pale.

"I'm sorry. I didn't mean to scare you. Was I going too fast?"

"Going fast was the whole point, I suppose."

He looked a little surprised when she unsnapped her belt and leaned across the console to hug him tightly.

"Thank you, thank you, thank you," she repeated as she pressed feverish kisses against his neck and jaw.

"I guessed that driving fast and free on the Dan Ryan would be the equivalent of foreplay for you. I'm just glad the feeling is transferring to me," he chuckled.

"Oh, it transferred to you all right," Esa assured him with a soft growl as she bit at his earlobe. "You have no idea what you just unleashed."

He grinned broadly but his hand on her jaw was firm as he gently pushed her back so that he could look into her eyes.

"I had an idea. But let's get one thing straight, honey."

"What?" Esa asked impatiently. Her nostrils flared to catch his delicious male scent. She couldn't take her eyes off his firm lips. She noticed that they set into a determined line when she tried to crane over to kiss him. He fingers burrowed into her hair and tightened, restraining her.

"Here in the car you're the boss. But up there my bedroom I'm in the driver's seat. Understood?"

Heat simmered between her thighs. She squirmed restlessly in the seat but Finn quirked one eyebrow...waiting.

"Yes, all right," she murmured, recognizing that he expected a verbal agreement.

He smiled. "Okay, let's go."

Esa wondered if Finn was testing her.

He'd led her into his bedroom and set her down on the edge of this bed. Then he'd said he would be right back and gone into the bathroom. Esa glanced around the dim bedroom in rising anticipation and nervousness.

It was almost the precise same scenario as that first night...the night she'd run out on him.

Like that night, she stood hesitantly and fiddled with her coat. She jumped when the bathroom door suddenly opened and she saw Finn's shadow outlined in the doorway. He'd left on the lights over the mirror in the bathroom so she could make out that he wasn't wearing anything but his low-riding jeans. His fly was partially unfastened. The erotic sight of the thin trail of golden-brown hair that ran from his taut bellybutton down below the waistband of his starkly white boxer briefs left Esa temporarily speechless.

"What are you doing?" he asked as he padded into the room with silent stealth. "Were you planning on running out again?"

"No!" Esa assured him when she heard the incredulity in his tone. She swallowed thickly. She didn't know why she was so nervous. It wasn't as if she'd never slept with him before.

Maybe her anxiety was due to that taut challenge he'd issued her in the parking garage. Maybe it was caused by the fact that she'd accepted it.

Perhaps she trembled with nerves and wild excitement because tonight it wasn't the same with Finn. The playful, fun, delicious near-stranger had disappeared. At some point he'd transformed into a fierce, determined, dead-sexy lover.

"I was…was starting to undress," Esa admitted in a hushed tone as he came toward her.

He grabbed her hand and swung her around while he seated himself on the bed. "Good. I can watch you."

Her heartbeat began to throb in her ears in the seconds that followed. His face looked sober and set.

"I…uh, well, I—"

He interrupted her stammering with a firm command.

"Take off your clothes, Esa."

Her hands shook a little, betraying her nervousness as she shrugged out of her leather jacket and tossed it on the floor. She'd never stripped for a man before. Surely Finn was going to be disappointed in her lack of seduction skills. But Esa just couldn't see herself morphing into slinky-stripper mode and giving him sultry winks as she tossed her panties into his lap.

Somehow she knew the sex kitten role would ring glaringly false tonight. Just as it should, perhaps. Esa craved to be herself with Finn as much as she feared that he would be turned off when he realized she wasn't really as experienced with no-strings-attached sexual affairs as she'd led him to believe.

She certainly didn't feel like much of a seductress as she unzipped her short boots and stripped off her socks, letting them fall limply to the carpet. Nevertheless Finn sat utterly motionless as he watched her every movement.

His gaze trailed her fingers when they rose to unbutton the pumpkin-colored sweater she wore. She knew the color flattered her skin tone, hair and eye color. Esa also recalled the way she'd caught Finn staring at her chest with a gleam of masculine appreciation in his eyes several times that evening. The sweater didn't cling to her indecently but it certainly left little to the imagination in regard to the shape and size of her breasts.

That recollection gave her confidence as she parted the two sides of the fabric and gave him a peek at the valley between her black lace-encased breasts. He tensed. His nostrils flared noticeably. Sexual excitement seemed to flood into her veins at the sight, quickening her flesh and sharpening her senses. Her fingers smoothed down the bare strip of exposed skin to her jeans and curled beneath the waistband.

"Take the sweater all the way off," Finn ordered abruptly.

Esa hesitated only for as long as it took her to recall her agreement in the parking garage earlier. Well a deal *was* a deal, after all.

The sweater dropped to the floor.

Finn leaned forward slightly in his sitting position. Her nipples tightened beneath his palpable stare as though he'd just reached out and caressed the tips.

"Now the jeans," he instructed after a tense moment.

Her fingers flew over her button fly at first, until she noticed how Finn's pulse leapt at his throat. Her movements slowed as she unfastened the buttons just over her most sensitive, aching flesh. Seemingly of their own accord her hips gyrated, circling subtly against her hand.

Esa bit her lip to still a moan at the subtle, evocative pressure. How many times in her life had she unbuttoned her jeans? And never once had it ever felt so tantalizingly sexual as it did with Finn's hot eyes watching her.

Finn's gaze shot up from where it had been glued to her crotch.

"Stop teasing me, Esa," he said in a hard tone.

"I wasn't—"

"Take off those jeans. Now."

Esa wasted no time in shoving the jeans down her hips and shimmying out of them. When she stood in front of him wearing just her bra and panties she saw that Finn was in the process of unfastening the rest of his own button flies. The glimpse of the thick pillar of his cock pressing tightly against the white cotton of his underwear made Esa reach hastily for her panties.

"No. Turn around to take them off," Finn demanded.

Esa turned around slowly, not because she was trying to be seductive but because she wasn't overly thrilled about him getting an eyeful of all her bountiful flesh. She paused in wide-eyed disbelief while in the process of pulling her silk panties over her bottom when she heard him groan behind her.

"God, you're sexy, honey."

Esa clenched her eyes shut, taken by surprise by the emotion that crashed through her at what she'd heard in his tone. She bent and drew her panties over her thighs. By the time she'd stepped out of them she'd gained a measure of control over her feelings.

She turned to face him with a newfound pride. That's what the sound of the pure, raw desire in Finn's deep voice had given her just now. She stood still while his gaze ran over her belly and hips, lingering between her thighs, scorching her in the process. When he just nodded once toward her chest, seemingly incapable of speaking for the moment, she unfastened her bra and slipped it off her shoulders.

"Come here," he said hoarsely after a moment.

Chapter Fifteen

∞

Esa walked toward him, her heart hammering loudly in her ears, pausing just inside his spread thighs. She made a little strangled sound of arousal when he put his hands on her waist and pulled her to him. She stared down at him in helpless desire as his blond head moved forward. His nose and lips almost skimmed the skin of her stomach...almost. He remained a fraction of an inch away from her as he moved his head over her and inhaled deeply.

"*Finn,*" she groaned, completely a prisoner of her desire at that moment.

"I love the way you smell," he muttered, more to himself than to her. He planted a single hot kiss on her bellybutton. Her abdominal muscles quivered in longing at the simple caress. Her fingers came up to tangle in his soft collar-length hair as he pressed his lips along her stomach and hips, tasting her occasionally with his agile tongue, taking love bites from her curving flesh. His hands lowered to explore her buttocks, shaping and molding her into his palms.

If another man had been doing it, Esa likely would have felt self-conscious about her body. But Finn's warm, cherishing mouth and caressing hands made her feel so rich in her femininity, so soft, so beautiful.

When he scraped his teeth along a lower rib her nipples pulled unbearably tight. Before she knew what he was about he grabbed her wrists and pushed her hands toward her breasts.

"Hold them up for me," he said, his light blue eyes gleaming silver in the dim light as he looked up at her.

She hesitated only a second before she gathered her breasts in her hands, cradling them from below. Her face tightened with mixed arousal and poignant emotion when he leaned forward and slipped an erect nipple between his lips.

He watched her for a moment as he drew on her breast so sweetly. She clamped her thighs together to still the ache he wrought. His tongue was a warm, abrasive lash one second, a sleek soothing glide the next. Her hands trembled around her breasts. She closed her eyes and moaned when he transferred his mouth to her other nipple and moved his hands to the backs of her thighs. He reached into the tight crevice, coaxing her to part for him.

"*Ohhhh,*" Esa cried out in helpless abandon when he slid a finger into her slit. He lifted his head a fraction of an inch from her glossy, erect nipple.

"You're so wet," he praised, his voice thick with lust.

Without consciously realizing she did it, Esa plumped her breasts in her hands, offering herself to him for further ravishment. He accepted her offer eagerly, dipping his head and drawing on her nipple with a steady, firm suction, palming her left buttock and lifting her flesh in order to make an easier passage for a second finger.

Esa's eyes shot open when he worked the first well-lubricated finger through her labia and rubbed her moist, sensitive tissues. Moments later the simmering fire in her flesh flashed into a blinding explosion.

"Shhhh," Finn whispered softly as his lips brushed against her temple. Esa blinked in disorientation. She was lying on her back on Finn's bed and he leaned over her, still wearing his unfastened jeans. Her breath passed raggedly over her lips in the aftermath of her orgasm.

"Oh my God, that felt so good," she mumbled as her hands rose to touch his beautiful golden body. She could feel his hard penis pressed against her thigh. It emanated heat, driving her wild. She reached for him.

But he thwarted her attempts by grabbing both her wrists and pushing them to the mattress above her head.

"What are you doing?" she asked, miffed at being denied the treat of caressing his lean, well-defined muscles gloved in thick, smooth skin or stroking his long, shapely cock.

"I'm tired of your teasing me all the time. I told you I was the boss here in bed." Although his look was hard, his lips curved into a sexy grin. "And the boss says you have to keep your hands above your head."

"Or?"

"You don't want to find out," he told her pointedly. Esa rolled her eyes.

But she didn't move her hands.

Instead she lay there in growing trepidation and anticipation as he knelt between her knees and deliberately spread her thighs wide. Her hips shifted restlessly.

"Finn…"

"Yes?" he asked as he looked up at her.

Esa swallowed heavily. She experienced a strange brew of paradoxical emotions. She wanted to close her legs and lower her hands to cover her vulnerable core. She also felt a powerful desire to remain spread like that for Finn—stretched open wide. Her fingers clutched desperately to each other when he began to lean down over her, his eyes on her face.

"I-I don't think that—"

"I *do* think. No running this time, Esa," he told her softly. He opened his large hands on her thighs, keeping her spread wide, and lowered his head.

And Esa forgot how to breathe.

She stared up at the ceiling wide-eyed, seeing nothing as sensation flooded her awareness. Nothing could distract her from the intense feelings that Finn's firm, agile tongue or sublime suction wrought on her flesh. He'd taken away all possibility of action, holding her firmly so that her hips couldn't squirm away from his exquisite, deliberate torture. She couldn't even hold his head to her, cherish him, attenuate the pressure when it became overwhelming.

She just had to take it. And it was so, *so* good.

Finn growled low and feral a while later when she arched up off the bed, her muscles flexing almost unbearably tight as she came. He nursed her through the roughest part of her storm while she cried out and whimpered and her fingernails pressed crescent shapes into her palms.

She watched through heavy eyelids as he rose up over her and dove for the bedside table. Her body throbbed with a dull, heavy ache. When Finn shoved his jeans and underwear to his thighs she realized just how aroused he was. He wasted no time in sliding on a condom and positioning himself.

She cried out sharply when he arrowed into her in one stroke, hard and true. He shouted out simultaneously and dropped his cheek to her shoulder, pressing his lips to her neck. Esa waited anxiously as her body accustomed itself to his presence and Finn's warm breath struck her in rapid puffs of air. He lifted his head slowly when she caressed his shoulders and back.

"Put your arms back on the bed, Esa," he ordered.

Her eyes went wide. She slowly replaced her hands above her head on the bed.

His cock throbbed inside her.

He came up off her upper body, leaning on his muscular arms. Esa panted shallowly as he pinned her with his stare and began to move.

After a moment, Esa closed her eyes. It was really too much for her to bear. Pleasure swamped her. His cock filled her so perfectly, rubbing and agitating deep, secret, virgin flesh. But it wasn't just that. Watching him as he watched her, feeling him merge with her so completely…it felt like the most intimate moment she'd ever experienced.

And Esa didn't know what to make of that.

He allowed her the small escape of shutting her eyes for a while as he built the friction in her all over again. But then he changed the angle of his assault on her senses and slammed into her more forcefully.

"Open your eyes," she heard him demand in an uneven, rough voice.

She followed his command, her face clenching with desire at the sight of him. He held his long, lean beautiful body off her with his hands on the headboard behind her. Their pelvises smacked against each other briskly with each downward plunge of his long, deliberate thrusts. His golden torso gleamed with a coat of perspiration.

When she looked into his heavy-lidded gaze his formerly smooth, long strokes became delicious, fast jabs. His handsome face tightened at the amplified pleasure.

"Come, Esa. Come with me."

Esa jerked her head back and screamed, submitting to his command without conscious thought, climaxing powerfully. Finn roared as he joined her. He continued to pump into her hard and fast throughout his own orgasm, the sensation of his spasming, thrusting cock giving her the longest, most explosive orgasm she'd ever experienced in her life.

He collapsed on top of her, panting heavily. Esa finally moved her arms, stroking his back languorously, loving the feel of his weight on her and the bursts of his breath on her shoulder. Eventually his ragged gasps slowed and evened and he resituated himself more comfortably on top of her. He groaned when she lightly scraped his skin with her nails.

A heavy, warm sensation settled into Esa's limbs. She felt her body sinking...sinking further into the mattress, further into this drowsy, delicious fog.

"Finn?" she muttered sleepily.

He lifted his head to look at her.

"You were right," she whispered. She saw him quirk up one brow slightly in query. "I should let you have the driver's seat more often. At least when we're not in a car."

Esa struggled to keep her eyelids open in order to see his growing smile.

"Esa?"

"Yes," she mumbled.

"Go to sleep."

"Okay."

And just like that she did.

The sun shone brightly through Finn's floor-to-ceiling windows when Esa blinked her eyes open groggily the next morning. She stirred lazily, only to sit up when she realized Finn wasn't in bed with her. She'd slept without dreams last night, warm and content within the circle of his arm.

At dawn she'd awakened to see his gaze on her. They'd made love again, slowly and sweetly, and in the end with a wild, intense abandon.

Afterward Esa had stared out the window as panic rose slowly in her breast. Eventually she'd joined Finn again in sleep. But this time her rest had been haunted by anxious dreams.

She was falling in love with him. Last night had signaled the treacherous moment when she crossed that line that led from cautionary infatuation to dangerous devotion.

Esa groaned softly and fell back on the bed.

She must have fallen under some kind of spell last night to let down her guard so completely. Maybe there was magic in the air on All Hallow's Eve. Because in the blazing light of day the events of last night—the memories of their passionate, soulful lovemaking—took on the quality of a dream.

It hurt knowing that while she'd fallen for him for all his wonderful characteristics, he'd given no clear indication that he cared for anything besides the convenient mutual sexual gratification that was behind their initial hook-up, an opportunity for some self-soothing rebound sex.

But surely there was more to it than that for him. Last night—his touch, his intensity, the raw need in his tone when he'd said her name.

All things that were easily ascribable to lust, Esa reminded herself grimly.

She jumped when the bathroom door opened. She was surprised to see that Finn had showered and dressed. He looked thoroughly edible in a pair of faded jeans and a light blue t-shirt that highlighted his lean, muscular torso, healthy tan and brilliant blue eyes to breathtaking effect.

"Do you have to go in to work?" she murmured when he came over to the bed and sat down.

He nodded before he leaned down and gifted her with one of his slow, hot, patentable kisses.

"I don't want to but I need to—at least for part of the day. We have a lot to do before we open that express lane for Monday morning traffic," he said softly next to her lips a few seconds later.

"It seemed just perfect to me."

"Monday morning traffic is a bit more complicated to consider than one red-headed speed demon in a Ferrari," he teased her warmly. He delved his fingers in her hair and studied the way it looked in his hand for a silent moment. "You were going to tell me something about a misunderstanding last night. Remember?"

"Oh, right. I guess I forgot with everything else that happened," Esa said, trepidation jolting through her at his unexpected words.

He met her gaze and smiled. "It's okay. You sort of made me forget about everything else too. So what was it that you wanted to tell me?"

Esa swallowed uneasily. "It...it actually all started with that car."

His forehead scrunched in confusion. "The car? Your Ferrari?"

"Well the thing about it is, see, it's not really *my* car. Those license plates and everything—SXKITN69. *As if,*" Esa rolled her eyes, her nervousness increasing when Finn's gaze narrowed on her. "And—you'll think this part is funny," she said, although the last thing Finn looked like doing at that moment was laughing, "I'm not really the publisher of *Metro Sexy* magazine."

"Why did you tell me you were, then?"

"Well, I never really did. You just *assumed* that."

He gave her a strange, unreadable look and straightened. "I assumed that because your name was on the office door and you were sitting behind your desk."

Esa bit her lip anxiously as she sat up in bed, securing the sheet around her breasts. It sounded even worse than she'd expected when she said it out loud. But she'd started now—she couldn't stop. "That's not my office. It's my sister Rachel's office. Everybody calls *her* Kitten. It's her Ferrari. *She's* the publisher of *Metro Sexy*. My offices are actually in Orland Park. I'm a physician."

"You're a physician," Finn repeated flatly.

Esa nodded, not caring for the toneless quality of his voice. This was not going as well as she'd hoped.

"Your offices are in Orland Park," he said, as though he were trying to get everything straight. "And yet I specifically remember you telling me some story about driving north in traffic that first night because you wanted to start a south suburban version of *Metro Sexy*."

Esa grimaced. "Well, I had to say *something*—"

"And that something was a lie," he clarified slowly.

"Well, yes, but—"

"What part of it was true then?" His eyes raked over the mussed bed before he stood.

"Finn, don't ask that. Of course all the important stuff was...you know. Genuine." She watched him in rising panic as he studied her, almost feeling him flying away from her, distancing himself even though he hadn't moved, technically speaking. God, here he was bruised and shaken from the likes of Julia Weatherell and she pelted something like this at him. Esa suddenly felt as if she'd rattled his Self-Confidence Richter Scale like King Kong.

"I-I thought it was what you wanted."

His nostrils flared slightly as he broke their stare. "Why would I want to be lied to?"

"You're taking this all wrong. Let me explain—"

"Actually, I don't have time for it right now, Esa. I need to get to work."

Esa just stared in open-mouthed incredulity as he walked out of the room. A few seconds later she heard the front door open and shut with what sounded to her ringing ears like a grim click of finality.

* * * * *

"Are you sure you want to trade?" Rachel asked as she dangled the keys to Esa's Lexus teasingly in front of her sister's face.

They stood out on the driveway of their parents' home. Both the dark blue Lexus and the red Ferrari gleamed brightly in the bright autumn sunlight. David Ormond finished winding the hose that they'd used to wash both cars and stood.

"I'm going inside to catch the end of the Illinois game," Esa's father said.

"Thanks for the help, Dad," Esa called as he waved and walked toward the house.

"Go Illini!" Rachel cheered in her best macho voice.

Esa and Rachel often went out to their parents' suburban house to wash their cars since they both had indoor parking spots in the city. Even though the day was chilly they'd decided to wash their cars before they returned them back to their original owners. Unfortunately they hadn't been able to talk much while they did it since their father was there helping.

"Well? What do you think? I'm betting you don't want to let go of my little pretty," Rachel teased.

"Don't be ridiculous," Esa mumbled distractedly as she grabbed her car keys. She'd been completely out of it all day. Her mind kept replaying the incident with Finn until she thought she'd scream if she pictured the way he'd looked at her one more time, as if she were a slightly revolting stranger who had suddenly appeared in his bed out of nowhere.

He just needed some time to process it. He had a right to be a bit dazed after learning she'd lied to him, after all.

What if he never wanted to talk to her again?

Esa found herself staring at the shiny cherry red Ferrari. It was all that stupid car's fault.

"It was a nightmare driving that thing, you know," she told Rachel sourly. "That car is like giving a double dose of Viagra to every horn-dog in the city."

Rachel chuckled. "Horn-dog? Is *that* what you'd call Finn Madigan?"

Esa did a double take and grabbed her sister's elbow. "Come on. Let's go for a walk," she said sternly.

"Uh oh. Am I in trouble, teacher?"

Esa studied her little sister through narrowed eyelids. At the moment she looked almost exactly like she had when she was fifteen years old, when she'd made it her life's mission to tease and torment every waking moment of Esa's anguished teenage years. Her dark red hair was pulled into a high, bouncy ponytail. She wore faded jeans and white Keds tennis shoes. Her pretty face looked fresh-scrubbed as a dewy peach in the bright sunlight. Few would have guessed that the young woman who walked next to Esa with the mischievous glint in her big brown eyes had single-handedly launched and ran the most popular magazine in the city of Chicago.

"Carla spilled that you plotted with her for this whole *flirting in traffic* scheme, even getting me to drive that pimpette machine of yours to further your cause."

Rachel smiled in a friendly fashion, completely unscathed by the fury in her sister's tone. "I'd love to take all the credit but in all fairness I can't. I wanted you to loosen up a little, have some fun, that's all. Both Carla and I have been worried that you were going to pre-purchase your cemetery plot any day now. But you far surpassed my expectations, Esa. Who'd a thought you'd actually snag yourself a man as gorgeous as Finn Madigan?

"His *brother* though," Rachel paused and made a sound of disgust, "I feel terrible that Carla got hooked up with such a loser. A few more dating nightmares like hers and *Metro Sexy's* reputation is going straight down the drain."

Esa refrained from sarcastically expressing the great loss to the world *that* would be. All of the fury and confusion about what had occurred with Finn this morning found a focused outlet on her sister.

"For your information, Carla is crazy about Jess. It's *my* situation that's a nightmare, and *Metro Sexy's* got nothing to do with that. No, that's all *your* fault! You never could keep your nose out of my life. Just like that time you called Blake Merrill when I was in the tenth grade and told him I was crying my eyes out in my bed because he'd broken up with me."

"I was pissed off at that jerk. I wanted him to know what an idiot he was for dumping my sister," Rachel defended.

Esa stopped in front of Mr. and Mrs. Burbage's brick colonial and turned to face her sister. "I was mortified. The last thing I wanted was for Blake to know how I really felt about him when he'd broken up with me!"

"And then he asked out that sleazy Marianne Jordan, remember?"

"Rachel, that's not the point!" Esa shouted so loud that Mr. Burbage pushed back the curtains and looked outside. Rachel waved in a friendly fashion before she grabbed Esa's elbow and forced her to start walking.

"And why in the world didn't you tell me about Finn's calling you?" Esa asked, her voice shaking with anger. She was at least mollified to see that Rachel looked a bit guilty.

"Oh, that. Well, I was confused at first—I mean, who was this guy calling me and saying he was concerned about me leaving and was everything all right, and would I please give him a call? I didn't recognize his name and I haven't gone on any benders for at least a month, so I knew I couldn't have just blacked it out," Rachel added with a gamine grin that faded when Esa gave her an exasperated look.

"Right. So the next thing I know he's calling and mentioning not only your name, but Julia Weatherell's. Well, *that* got my interest."

"What did he say, precisely?" Esa asked, her footsteps slowing.

"He said he felt bad about Julia just walking into the bedroom like that." Rachel paused and gave her sister an openly curious look.

"Go on," Esa grated out.

Rachel sighed, obviously recognizing she wasn't going to get anything juicy out of her dried-up older sister.

"He said that he and Julia used to be engaged and that apparently she felt she had the right to enter his condominium any time she pleased. 'Which she doesn't'—that's what he said, rather firmly, I should add."

"Really?" Esa asked slowly, unable to disguise her obvious interest in the news.

Rachel nodded, ponytail bobbing.

"He also said that he wished you'd stop running out on him. He sounded downright pissed about it."

Esa colored hotly and picked up the pace.

"What did he mean by that? Why do you keep running out on him?" Rachel queried as she jogged to keep up with Esa like she was a reporter hot on the trail of the story of a lifetime.

"What would you have done if you were in bed with a guy who you knew for one night and his ex-fiancée walked in on you?"

"So you *did* go to bed with Finn?" Rachel asked, triumph gleaming in her liquid brown eyes. She flinched back when Esa swung around wildly.

"Is that all you care about? Is sex all *anybody* cares about?"

"Well, it's a good place to start, isn't it?" Rachel asked simply.

Esa's breath popped out of her lungs. For once she couldn't argue with her little sister's logic. Sex and desire was as good a place as any to start something.

At least it was if the desire was based on honesty —

"I know you must like Finn, Esa." Rachel interrupted her thoughts. "Otherwise you wouldn't have blown a gasket when I said I'd gone to the party last night to find out if Finn would tell me more details about Julia's extracurricular activities."

"For your magazine," Esa added with a frown.

"Yes, for *Metro Sexy*," Rachel agreed with a stubborn tilt to her chin. "I am a journalist you know, and despite your high and mighty attitude, Julia Weatherell bedding down with other guys when she's leading around Gavin Graves Jr. like she's got a hook through his nose is big news. He's one of the most eligible bachelors in the city, you know. Carla filled me in on all the details about her and Finn this morning when we met for breakfast at The Mighty Nice Café."

Esa scowled, although she wasn't really angry at Carla for breeching her confidence. It must have been obvious to Carla that Rachel was already in on the secret about Julia due to Finn's mistaken phone call.

"Julia didn't sleep with Finn. At least not recently. And under no circumstances *whatsoever* are you to bring up that incident in Finn's condo in your gossip column," Esa repeated what she'd whispered so heatedly last night.

"I told you I wouldn't. Let's turn back. The further we go the longer I'll have to put up with you lecturing me."

They walked silently for a half minute while Esa's emotions frothed and boiled. She didn't know why she was so furious at Rachel. Her sister's behavior in this case wasn't that different than it had been dozens of times in the past. She knew Rachel loved her with a fierce loyalty. Even if she did occasionally make Esa's life a living hell, Esa loved her just as much in return.

"I hope you don't sabotage the whole thing."

Esa glanced over at Rachel in surprise. "What's that supposed to mean?"

"Simple. Ever since you first started dating boys you were convinced that the really cute, nice ones didn't like you. Even when they clearly were leching after you, you were always sure that at any moment they were going to fall for a slut or a skinny cheerleader."

"That's because they usually did."

"Maybe a few of them did," Rachel conceded. "There's always going to be some rotten apples in the bunch. Doesn't mean you should stop eating fruit altogether."

"Profound analogy, Kitten," she muttered drolly.

Esa suddenly felt exhausted when they turned up her parents' driveway. Her fingers found her car keys in her jacket pocket. A heavy weight seemed to press down on her as she stared at her sedate sedan. A dependable car, luxurious yet conservative. A doctor's car. The vehicle of a practical, reasonable woman.

"Are you sure you don't want to trade again for awhile?" Rachel asked from beside her.

Esa swallowed the ache of longing in her throat. She hated to admit that she'd loved driving that fast little car. It seemed so juvenile of her, so out of character. And when she thought of the gift that Finn had given her, of flying swift and unhindered into the city last night with him by her side, she was *so* tempted to take her sister up on her offer.

Just like she was wild with a hunger to find out if this thing she had with Finn could be more than just a sexy fling.

"Absolutely not," Esa said with a brisk fortitude she was far from feeling. She paused in the process of walking toward her car and glanced over her shoulder. "But thanks for asking, anyway."

Rachel gave her a warm smile. "If you like Finn, don't give up. The thing about a chance is that you've got to take it, Esa. Otherwise it'll just become a regret."

"There are no guarantees that it won't end up being a regret if I do take a chance," Esa said doubtfully, secretly thinking that maybe she'd already blown that chance.

"It's not a sure thing, that's true," Rachel replied. "But just like *Metro Sexy* always reminds its readers, regret *is* guaranteed if you don't try."

As Esa drove down Lake Shore Drive ten minutes later—the experience notably less thrilling in her bulky, dependable car—she thought about what Rachel had said in regard to taking chances and regrets. She had to admit that Rachel's advice sounded pretty darn sound, even if it did come from the mouth of a gossip columnist.

Chapter Sixteen

Finn frowned when he came home later and saw his neatly made bed. What had he expected, that Esa would still be there, warm and soft and naked? After the way he'd walked out on her earlier following her disturbing revelation?

Not bloody likely, he thought grimly as he tossed his keys onto the dresser.

He'd been restless and unsettled for the better part of the morning. What kind of a game was she playing, lying so blatantly about herself? he wondered for the thousandth time that day.

He scowled and started peeling off his clothes. What he needed was a good long run beside the lake followed by a workout at his gym. The exercise would help him clear his thoughts and give him the space he needed so he could stand back and examine the situation with Esa more clearly.

Maybe he should ask out another woman tonight. Or perhaps he'd take Caleb up on his offer and meet him at a sports bar this evening to watch the Ohio State-Michigan game. His fixation on Esa wasn't healthy, Finn decided as he took the underground pedestrian tunnel beneath Lake Shore Drive a short while later. He'd just come out of a bad breakup. He hardly knew her.

Plus, she was a god-damned liar.

Given all those strikes against her it was a no-brainer. He should forget about Esa Ormond.

Wasn't it a common enough occurrence for a guy to become seriously infatuated after being burned in a relationship? Finn thought as he ran next to a brilliant cerulean blue Lake Michigan. He'd seen it happen to friends in the past.

The excitement, the challenge and the hot and heavy sex helped to shore up a wounded self-esteem.

A slender, attractive blonde woman jogging in the opposite direction from him gave him an appreciative once-over. He returned her blatantly obvious grin of invitation. He'd gone another half mile before he realized that he'd just passed up the perfect opportunity to ask out another woman, and all because he'd been too preoccupied in enumerating the reasons he shouldn't think about Esa anymore.

Damn.

After he'd returned from his health club and showered he'd eyed his cell phone on the bedside table. He'd probably be able to reach her now that he understood that she wasn't Kitten Ormond but *Dr. Esa* Ormond.

A complete stranger.

He rolled his eyes and cursed under his breath as he reached for his phone. It pissed him off to know that all of his head-clearing and rationalizations hadn't helped one iota. He still wanted her. He cursed his overactive libido but he couldn't stop thinking about how fantastic it had been making love to her last night, how sweet to hold her afterward while she slept — that small, satisfied smile still shadowing her lips.

I should let you have the driver's seat more often. At least when we're not in a car.

He rapidly reached for his phone. Since when had he become so fricking desperate? He thought with a scowl. His hasty fingers paused on the keypad when he heard someone knock at his front door.

He hit the disconnect button on his phone.

Julia stood in the hallway looking pale and tense. She wore a pair of tight black pants that hugged her trim thighs and an ivory cashmere sweater. Her dark, sleek hair hung long and loose, making a striking contrast against the ivory wool. Her fitted pants were tucked into a pair of supple leather boots.

It struck Finn that while he still appreciated Julia's elegance and beauty—there were few men who wouldn't—he was no longer compelled by it like he used to be. He certainly no longer experienced the intense lust that used to flood him at the sight of her. He realized for the first time that the emotion he associated most with her was a sense of nostalgia for what could have been more than for what *was*, grief for the loss of a fantasy as insubstantial as smoke.

"What is it?" he asked, referring to her anxious face and rigid posture.

He saw her throat convulse as she swallowed. "We need to talk. It's important."

Finn just nodded once and closed the door after her. She didn't speak until she'd entered the living room and turned to him. He didn't think he'd ever seen her so tense during the length of their relationship.

"One of my friends overheard Kitten Ormond talking at The Mighty Nice Café this morning. She *knows* about us, Finn. If she goes public with it in that rag *Metro Sexy* Gavin Graves will drop me."

Finn's brow crinkled in confusion at the near panic that laced her tone. "I don't understand. You have a friend who overheard *what*? There's nothing to tell about *us*."

Julia's face paled even further.

"Do you think I don't know that?" she hissed. "Do you have to throw it in my face that you rejected me? Kitten Ormond is the city's biggest gossip. She'd do anything to ruin me. Do you think she cares about the truth? She *knows* about me coming here! She knows that I wanted to…" Julia hesitated briefly before her chin went up defiantly. "I suppose you told Esa about the time before, how I suggested that we continue to sleep together?"

"Hold on a second," Finn said sharply. He was bewildered by the turn of events but he understood this particular accusation loud and clear. Finn was very private about his life. He didn't kiss and tell about anyone he became involved with, let alone the woman he'd planned to marry. "I told Esa no such thing. I wouldn't run off at the mouth about something like that."

Julia only looked partially mollified. "Well, Esa has undoubtedly drawn her own conclusions given what she saw. The Ormond sisters have been jealous of me for years. They'd love to see my name smeared all over the gossip columns. When Gavin hears about it he's going to be *furious*. My reputation is going to be ruined. You've got to promise me that you'll try to stop it. I'm not the only one whose name is going to be dragged through the mud, you know."

Finn stared incredulously. Surely Esa wouldn't put the private details of his life out there for public consumption.

Would she?

How the hell do I know what Esa would do? He thought with a cold blast of reality. Until this morning he hadn't even known what she did for a living. He was just a casual fling, after all.

It might be Julia's story but it was *his* as well. Esa had no right to it, nor did her gossipmongering little sister.

"Finn?" Julia shrilly interrupted his thoughts. "Did you know she was planning on doing this?"

"Of course not," he replied.

"I should have known something like this would happen ever since I walked in here and saw you with Esa." She shook her head and growled through clenched teeth in sheer frustration. "God, I hate the Ormond sisters. Since when did you acquire such abysmal taste in women?"

The fury that swept through him at Julia's attack on Esa gave Finn the biggest shock of a day already filled with surprises. He'd never seen Julia behave this way, not even when she was outraged with him for taking over his father's business. It was like she'd just removed a mask and shown him what she really looked like.

And the sight wasn't a pretty one.

"Look, I don't know anything about this and I'd appreciate it if you stopped jumping all over me. From what I know about Esa she'd never consider doing what you're alleging."

"You're a *fool* if you believe that. She would expose me in a heartbeat. You don't know anything about it. She would love to ruin my chances with Gavin. She and that viper sister of hers would laugh until they cried, and then one of them would likely try to scoop up Gavin on the rebound."

"You told me that you were miserable with him, that he couldn't begin to please you in bed. Why are you so worried about it?" Finn asked, referring to the night she'd accosted him in his lobby.

"Well, that may very well be but that doesn't mean I want the world to know it. I have a reputation to uphold."

"Maybe you should have thought of that before you cornered me in my lobby and begged me to fuck you."

"How dare you! I'll have you know that—"

"Stop," Finn said, interrupting her tirade. He couldn't really grasp everything that Julia had been saying but he knew one thing. This conversation was *over*. As far as he was concerned Julia's behavior this afternoon had created a big, fat period on the end of the chapter that had been their relationship.

When he told her so she stared at him in disbelieving rage for a few seconds.

"You never did have what it takes," she accused, her gimlet green eyes flashing with disdain. "I should have known from the beginning you would fold just when you got to the finish line of making a big name for yourself."

Finn shook his head slowly. How could he have possibly been so mistaken about a woman? He said the first thing that came to his head. "*God* I'm lucky. What if I hadn't seen this side of you until after I'd married you?"

Flirting in Traffic

She started as if he'd slapped her but Finn was beyond caring about her feelings, beyond caring about her one way or another. She'd been right about one thing. He *did* have abysmal taste in woman.

"It's time for you to leave."

She threw him a vitriolic look before she turned and left, slamming the door behind her as she went.

"Good riddance," Finn muttered under his breath. He sat down heavily on his couch, both his brain and blood running a mile a minute.

He got up abruptly after a while and stared at the darkening lake. The sun died a brilliant, fiery death in the west, casting bright orange reflections on the glass surfaces of the eastern high-rises. By the time it had completely set Finn's anger at Julia had largely calmed.

It wasn't her fault that he had crap taste in women, after all.

He picked up his cell phone and dialed directory assistance.

Chapter Seventeen

Esa kept herself busy for the rest of the afternoon cleaning her loft and catching up on work, trying not to fret about whether or not Finn would call, whether she should call him or if she should just forget about him altogether.

As if *that* was even a remote possibility.

At least after her talk with Rachel she felt better prepared to confront Finn again. Well, sort of — if this wild anticipation and trembling anxiety could be called better prepared.

When her phone did finally ring at around six-thirty she was so tense that she spasmodically jerked the medical file she'd been holding. Papers clattered and skittered onto the wood floor.

"Hello?" she asked, unable to fully disguise the tremor in her voice.

"Esa? It's Finn."

"Oh, hi. You got the right number this time," she attempted cheerfully, trying to ignore how the sound of his voice made her heart pound loudly in her ears. "How are you?"

Her brow furrowed in the brief silence that followed.

"Finn?" she prompted anxiously.

"Hmmm? Oh, yeah. Fine."

"Are you...are you still angry about the..."

"I'm not mad anymore, Esa."

She swallowed anxiously when she heard the flat, distant quality of his voice. "You never really gave me a chance to explain why I did it."

"I'm sure you had a stellar reason. That wasn't really why I was calling. I just spoke with Julia."

"Oh?" Esa asked with growing unease. "Did she stop by your condo again?"

"Yeah, she was really upset. It seems that someone she knows overheard your sister talking about running a story in *Metro Sexy* about Julia trying to start up things again with me while still involved with this guy she's dating...Graves."

Esa's mouth gaped open. She hadn't expected *this*.

"Finn...that's not true."

"That's what I told her. But I have to admit, Esa, after this morning I'm not really sure what to think about you."

"It's true that Rachel came to your mother's last night because of the information you accidentally left her on her phone about Julia. But I absolutely *forbade* her to do any story about Julia or you. I know how much you would hate that," Esa rushed to explain.

"Yeah. Well, it looks like I don't have any other choice but to take your word on that."

Esa grabbed reflexively at the back of the couch as if to brace herself against the jolt of pain that suddenly went through her.

This was it.

She could just tell by the tone of his voice. The brilliant, all-too-brief affair with Finn Madigan was over...history.

"You *can* take my word on it. Please, Finn. I know how what I said this morning must have really taken you by surprise but you can trust me," Esa said softly.

For a few silent seconds, as she waiting nervously for his response, she thought she might have gotten through to him. But she knew she hadn't even before he spoke because she heard the sound of frustrated defeat in his sigh.

"You know, the thing of it is I can't trust you. And it's not just because of you lying. I'm not ready for this, Esa."

Esa stared at the cushions of her couch blankly, seeing nothing, feeling like a vacuum of empty space had just opened up between her neck and belly.

"Oh. I see," she murmured, even though in truth she felt blinded by hurt. "Well, I guess that's it then."

"Yeah..."

Esa's heart leapt to life in her breast. Had that been uncertainty she heard tingeing his deep voice? She was kidding herself.

"Goodbye then," she said breathlessly. She hit the disconnect button quickly before she made a fool of herself by begging Finn to give her a second chance.

She wasn't sure how long she just stood there while her body tried to fend off the inevitable pain. Finally she cursed bitterly and hurled her phone onto the couch where it bounced up several feet off the taut cushion before settling.

Christ, Carla had been right. She really *did* have the ability to screw up something that could have been once-in-a-lifetime fantastic.

Chapter Eighteen

Two weeks later Esa walked out the emergency room exit of South Suburban Hospital with her head lowered, deep in thought. It was six-thirty on a Friday evening and the ER was packed with sick, annoyed, bored people. A virulent flu had been going around, one that worried Esa in regard to her elderly patients, who were so much more prone to dehydration than the younger, heartier portion of the population. Given the fact that many of them took several medications, dehydration tended to make the drug concentration too high in the bloodstream, causing myriad other physical problems.

That was why she'd had to hospitalize Mr. Ungar this evening. Carla had called earlier and left a message that she'd just take the train home since she wasn't sure how long Esa would be and a last minute prediction had been made for a snowstorm.

Esa saw through the automatic glass doors that led out of the emergency room that the snow had already begun. She suppressed a groan of frustration when she saw how heavy it was. It fell straight down with no wind to hinder it, already accumulating thickly on the roads.

Great. Just great. The first storm of the season and not only had it come exceptionally early in the year but it was just recently being picked up by the weather forecast. People hadn't had the opportunity to prepare for it and take the train into the city this morning. Add to that the factors of Friday evening and the Dan Ryan road construction and Esa saw all the components for a horrific traffic nightmare unfolding.

Maybe it all was fated, seeing as how it *was* Friday, November thirteenth, Esa thought with wry amusement.

"Esa!"

Her heart seemed to drop like a bowling ball into her gut. That voice—it had sounded like—

"Esa, I thought that was you," the tall, attractive man with tousled burnished-brown hair said as he rushed to meet her.

Her gaze lowered over the black leather jacket and a pair of long thighs and trim hips encased in a well-fitted pair of khaki pants—both articles of clothing that were part of a state trooper uniform.

"Caleb. For a second I thought you were Finn," she said blankly. Her disappointment felt like a palpable weight on her sagging shoulders.

He gave her a brilliant grin and stroked his chin with a black-gloved hand. "I shaved my goat. Probably look a bit like him without it."

Esa did her best to return his smile. Caleb was right. A strong family resemblance did exist between the two cousins. The sight of it made her wonder if she'd truly recovered from that electric, brief fling with Finn like she kept telling herself she had or if she was really worse off than on the night he'd told her he wasn't ready for a relationship and Esa had cried herself half-comatose.

"How have you been?" she asked as she straightened, trying to throw off the emotional weight that had settled on her like a lead cloak at the sight of a gorgeous Madigan male. "Not sick, I hope?"

"Nah, we brought in a guy who was whacked out on drugs and driving on the interstate. Not a good combination along with this crap," he said as he nodded toward the falling snow.

"I'll say. I'm about to go home in it. Thanks for making my drive a little safer."

"All in the line of duty," he assured her with a sexy grin. He shifted on his booted feet and glanced down at the hat he held in his hands. "So...have you seen much of Finn lately?"

Esa shook her head. "Not in several weeks. It was just a casual thing, you know."

His green-eyed gaze snapped up to her face. "Really?"

"Sure," she answered with what she hoped was careless disregard.

"He's been working his ass off on the road construction. I doubt he's had much time for dating. Jess said he's been going all Yoda on everyone, holing up like a monk. I spoke to Molly a few days ago and she said she'd hardly heard a peep from him since the party. I have to say it surprises me—you two not seeing each other. I got the impression that Finn really liked you. And vice-versa."

She forced a laugh. "Your cop instincts were way off then, I guess."

He moved his hat restlessly in his hands but this time his eyes remained fixed on her. "I can't say I'm sorry."

Esa gave him a startled look. "Why?"

He shrugged. "I really liked you the night we met at Grandma Glory's Halloween party," he stated bluntly.

"Oh," Esa replied awkwardly. She grasped for a change of topic and scolded herself for it even while she did it. Was she nuts? How many sane women would try to deflect a male as sexy as Caleb Madigan, especially when he regarded her with so much warmth and frank male appreciation?

"How is your grandmother?" she asked rapidly.

"She's doing great. I heard from Mary Kate that she went to that doctor that you referred her to and the new physician reduced her diabetes medication."

Esa gave a genuine smile. "I'm so glad to hear it. Listen, I better get going. The snow just keeps getting worse—"

She stopped speaking when he took a step closer to her. She could smell the leather from his jacket and the subtle remnants of his cologne. It was a very nice, admittedly sexy combination. But he didn't smell like spicy aftershave or the clean outdoors. Caleb's scent didn't make her go weak in the knees or make heat pool between her thighs.

In other words, he didn't smell like Finn.

She looked down rapidly to shield her disappointment in herself for having such irritating thoughts. Hadn't she expressly forbidden herself for the past several weeks to dwell on Finn?

"Esa?"

"Hmmm?" she asked, still staring at the snow-sodden, dirty entryway carpet to the ER.

"My cop instincts really weren't that far off, were they? At least when it comes to how you feel about my cousin?" When she didn't immediately answer he continued softly. "In other words, I probably shouldn't ask you out unless I'm feeling particularly masochistic, right?"

"Caleb, that's sweet of you to consider but—"

"My motives were purely selfish, Esa. No sweetness involved."

His sigh of disappointment brought her eyes up to his face.

Jeez, he was almost as gorgeous as Finn. *She* was the one who was masochistic around here. If she'd wanted clear evidence that what she'd felt for Finn was far beyond simple lust she'd just had it handed to her on a silver platter. If it had just been about a couple rounds of great sex with a yummy man, Caleb would undoubtedly fill the bill, in spades.

But she *didn't* want that. The knowledge hardly reassured her.

"It's okay, Esa," he said when he saw what must have been a desperate plea in her eyes for him not to ask her out mixed with a mute apology.

"I'm sorry, Caleb. It's just not a great time for me…"

He nodded good-naturedly. "Enough said. I understand."

"I'm not sure you do," she muttered uncomfortably. She stepped back when she realized he still stood close. "I'd better get going."

"I'll see you around."

Esa smiled and nodded her head as she turned. She was just being polite, of course. It would be strange indeed if she ran into Caleb Madigan again…unless he pulled her over to give her a speeding ticket.

That was entirely possible, of course.

"Hey, Esa," he called.

"Yeah?"

"Be extremely careful on the way home. It's getting really bad on the interstates but we hear the side streets are much worse. The snow is really wet and falling heavier in a shorter period of time than I've ever seen. Not only can't the plows keep up, unprepared for the storm as the Illinois Department of Transportation was, but even the cleared areas are turning slick and thick within twenty minutes after the plow passes. Add to all that the temperature is supposed to drop ten to fifteen degrees and the wind is going to pick up in the next few hours. The Dan Ryan is going to be a skating rink, but I wouldn't advise taking any of the alternative routes. The Cook County police are considering closing Stony Island."

Esa sighed. She's been taking the alternative route of Stony Island all week, ostensibly to avoid the Dan Ryan traffic, in reality to avoid the chance of seeing Finn. Driving Stony Island Avenue had been just as teeth-grinding of a traffic experience as the Dan Ryan.

"Thanks for the advice, Caleb. Good luck out there tonight."

"Thanks, you too," he said with one of those flashing Madigan smiles. "I have a feeling we're both going to need all the luck we can get. It's going to be one hell of a Friday the thirteenth."

Esa decided an hour and a half later, after having traveled a total of twelve miles on I-57, that she didn't need luck. She needed a miracle if she—or any of the other unfortunate individuals on the road tonight—was ever going to make it home in one piece. She gripped the steering wheel tightly and forced her tensed shoulder and back muscles to relax but it was difficult. Constant vigilance was required to drive in the swirl of snow that encapsulated her car in a cloud of near invisibility.

The snow was so thick on the road that driving either too fast or too slow was dangerous. She'd seen two cocky motorists going thirty-five miles per hour suddenly lose control, sliding into nearby lanes. Luckily the cars behind them were traveling slow enough to avoid colliding but they'd been near misses.

Drivers who hesitated and went too slow were just as bad off. The snow on the pavement had the consistency of an eight-inch-thick Dairy Queen Blizzard. A certain amount of momentum was required to plow through the thick mess.

Esa's eyes burned as she strained to see through the veil of the snow as it flickered back and forth from a barely translucent veil to an utterly opaque gray curtain. She turned off the traffic report as she ever so carefully navigated the ramp onto the Dan Ryan Expressway. She required every last bit of attention she possessed to manage the slippery stretch of curving road safely.

After being in Dan Ryan traffic for almost an hour she felt like screaming in frustration. There were three times as many cars there as compared to I-57. Because of the narrowed lanes due to road construction, things were ten times more dangerous.

And Esa had only to glance ahead and see the ocean of red brake lights to know that she was royally screwed. Some kind of forward acceleration was required in the rapidly accumulating snow. Once she was forced to stop she knew there was a good chance she'd be stuck.

Where the hell were the snow plows and the IDOT trucks? She'd seen so many cars marooned at this point that she'd lost track of the count.

"Damn. Plus one more," Esa mumbled to herself. A black sedan three cars in front of her and one lane over was stuck. The driver gunned the engine in a frantic attempt to get out of the thick furrow of slippery snow. He overdid it and the car's rear end swung crazily around, hitting a car in Esa's lane. She braked with a pumping motion and brought her car to a dreaded stop.

In the distance she saw a lime green IDOT truck also spinning its wheels in the snow and going absolutely nowhere, blocking the newly opened express lane that Finn had let Esa drive in on Halloween night. About ten men were unsuccessfully trying to push the large truck out.

Esa rifled through her purse and found a bottle of water. She sipped it, feeling like she was viewing some kind of slapstick comedy unfolding through her front window. The ten men scattered in every direction, including upward onto the top of the truck, as a car tried to stop unsuccessfully and slid into the IDOT vehicle in slow motion.

"This has got to be one for the Chicago record books," she muttered. All the cars she could see at this point, in every direction, had come to a standstill. They were all going to sit here helplessly while the snow buried them.

Esa set her water down hastily and reapplied the cap when she realized that chances were she wouldn't be able to use the bathroom for hours. She flipped on the radio and learned that the state police had just officially closed the Dan Ryan due to unsafe road conditions.

"Great, Caleb. Couldn't you have closed it *before* I got on it?" Esa muttered sourly. She picked up her cell phone, trying to decide who she should call first to complain—Carla, Rachel or her parents—when a figure running rapidly through the immobile cars caught her attention. Esa heard an outraged shout. Several people started to emerge from their cars directly in front of Esa, all of them staring at the running woman who had now reached the side of the road.

Esa unclipped her seat belt and opened her car door. Pellets of snow stung her face as she stood.

"What's going on?" Esa shouted to the middle-aged, balding man wearing a dark blue overcoat who had also gotten out of his car directly in front of her.

"Crazy woman. She took off her kid's clothes and was trying to bury the baby in the snow before that guy over there stopped her!"

"What?" Esa asked in bewilderment.

"I'm telling you it's true. Take a look. Storm must bring out all the loonies," the man said as he shook his head and turned back to watch the spectacle unfolding at the side of the road.

Esa closed her car door and stepped forward in the thick snow. What a mess. No wonder they were all stranded. A car couldn't maneuver in this deep, heavy slush.

The first thought that Esa had when she saw the weeping, hysterical woman at the side of the road holding a wailing, half-naked toddler was that the man had been correct in his estimation. She *must* be having some sort of psychotic episode.

"How's putting your kid in the cold snow supposed to help him if he's sick?" a tall man with his back to Esa, wearing a black parka with the hood up said, his voice muffled by the wind and swirling snow. He had his hand on the crying woman's shoulder in a restraining hold.

"Let go of me! He's going to die, you fool," the woman shrieked.

"He's not going to die," the man said more softly. He removed his hand from her shoulder slowly, as if waiting to see what she would do. When the woman just stared up at him in frightened bewilderment he began to unbutton his coat. "Why don't you let me wrap him in my coat? It's freezing out here and your son's clothing is all covered with snow by now."

"Better I put him in his clothes then," the woman wailed. She bent and picked up the tiny pants and jacket that had been tossed next to the waist-high bank of snow created by the plows. Her hand shook pitifully as she held up the snowy garments. "He's burning up, don't you see? I have a thermometer in the car. His temperature is a hundred and five degrees! We were taking him to the emergency room but that was hours ago. And we're stuck in this mess," the woman added miserably.

Esa pushed through a small semi-circle of several people who had gathered to witness the bizarre scene.

"Excuse me, ma'am? I'm a doctor. I'd like to be of assistance if I can."

Both the woman and the tall man standing next to her turned.

"Oh thank God! Yes, please help me. My little boy is burning up with fever. Explain to this man that he needs to be cooled off in the snow."

Esa stared in open-mouthed shock up into Finn's equally startled face. The hood had fallen partially back, revealing his singular, tousled blond hair. She probably would have recognized him immediately if the hood hadn't been covering it.

"Doctor?" the woman asked shakily.

Esa blinked. "Everything's going to be just fine, ma'am. Finn? If the offer of the coat still stands, it'd be greatly appreciated."

He just nodded his head once and shrugged out of the coat. She was glad to notice that he wore a thick insulated shirt beneath it. Esa reached for the crying, clearly miserable toddler. Finn stepped close and wrapped the child in his coat once Esa had the small, shivering boy in her arms.

"I know that a fever of one hundred and five is alarming, Ms.—"

"Angstrom. Toni Angstrom. And that's my boy Scott. My father and I were taking him to the hospital when we got caught in this storm."

Esa nodded as she made soothing sounds to the wailing child. "Like I was saying, a fever of a hundred and five is alarming, and you were right to want to take Scott to the hospital. But the chances are the doctors wouldn't have been able to do much. A fever is the body's natural defense, a way of making poor living conditions for the virus that Scott has caught. While a hundred and five degrees is a bad temperature, the best we can do for him at this point is make him as comfortable as possible until the bug runs its course."

"But my mother used to put me in a cold bath when I had a high fever! That's why I thought the snow..." The distraught woman waved at the snow bank.

Esa shook her head. "Sometimes doctors recommend a tepid bath but it's not a good idea to put a sick child in the ice-cold snow, Ms. Angstrom."

The woman's face crumpled.

"It's okay," Esa soothed. "Everything is going to be just fine. Now, why don't you show me to your car? Scott needs a nice comfortable place to rest right now."

"All right," she sniffled and passed in front of Esa.

Esa turned to Finn. She'd been aware of his steady gaze fixed on her during the entire exchange with Ms. Angstrom. Now that she'd had a moment to reflect back on it, she recognized his bulky clothing as belonging to one of the men that had been trying to push the IDOT truck out of the express lane.

"I know you're probably very busy with everything going on but would you mind coming? I may need some help."

"Sure," he replied gruffly.

Toni Angstrom led them to a white Oldsmobile. Esa instructed Toni to get back into the driver's seat. She said a quick hello to the elderly gentlemen who sat in the passenger seat as she settled a whimpering Scott in the back. Toni shakily introduced Esa and her father, Eli Shore, to one another.

Esa stood and squinted to see Finn's face through the swirling snow.

"My car is right over there," she said, pointing.

"Where?" he asked, obviously confused.

"There...the dark blue Lexus." She felt her cheeks color when he met her gaze steadily. Maybe he'd been looking for the Ferrari, she thought with a flash of embarrassment. "The keys are still in the ignition. If you could get them, my purse and my medical bag out of the trunk, I'd really appreciate it."

Finn nodded and started to go.

"Oh, and the bottle of water next to the driver's seat, please!" Esa called out. She really needed to try to get some fluid into the little boy. Finn turned and nodded once in understanding.

Esa clambered into the backseat of the Oldsmobile and closed the door. She spent the next minute trying to calm and comfort Toni Angstrom equally as much as the sick child. At one point Scott's grandfather turned with unnatural stiffness in his seat. Esa peered at him through the semi-darkness.

The back of her neck prickled a warning.

"Ms. Angstrom, can you please turn on the inside lights?" Esa asked.

"Certainly," the woman replied. She looked a little surprised when she did so and turned around to see the doctor staring not at her sick child but at her father.

"Are you feeling all right, Mr. Shore?" Esa asked, taking in his pale face tinged with a sickly shade of grayish-blue. He seemed barely able to turn around in his seat he held his shoulders and chest so stiffly. Pain pinched his features. As Esa watched, he clutched briefly at his left shoulder and winced.

The elderly gentlemen glanced uneasily at his daughter before he answered. Esa's heart went out to him. He was obviously worried about frightening the distraught woman any more than she already was.

"I'm doing just fine. Worried about my grandson, of course," he said in a thin, thready voice.

"Do you have a heart condition?" Esa asked softly.

His lips thinned. He nodded almost imperceptibly before Toni could turn her anxious gaze to him.

Esa gave what she hoped was a reassuring smile. Panic wouldn't do anyone any good at this point. "Try to relax, Mr. Shore. Your grandson is going to be just fine. You can turn down the lights, Mrs. Angstrom."

When she saw Finn approaching, Esa quickly got out of the car and shut the door behind her.

"What's wrong?" Finn said when he saw her face.

Esa reached quickly for the medical bag he carried along with her purse.

"Are there any lanes open at all for emergency medical vehicles?" she asked quietly.

His brow furrowed. "The express lane has been closed for emergency vehicle use only because of the storm. But you saw how they're fairing in this crap. They're getting stuck just as easily as the motorists they're supposed to be assisting," he said, referring to the IDOT truck he'd been trying to push out of the snow earlier with other members of his construction crew.

"You need to call for an ambulance. And Finn...you and your men need to find a way for it to get through. There's a medical emergency."

"Were you just saying all that stuff about the kid being okay to calm the mother down?" Finn asked intently.

Esa shook her head. "No. It's not Scott who needs immediate medical attention. It's his grandfather, Mr. Shore. I think he's either had a heart attack or is in the process of having one as we speak. Thank God I have aspirin in my bag, but there's not much else I can do except to keep his daughter from getting hysterical."

"Don't worry, Esa. We'll get the ambulance through."

She took reassurance from the steely fortitude of his tone. "*Shore*. Eli Shore. Tell them, there's a small chance they'll be able to pull up some records on him. And Finn, thank you," she said earnestly before she opened the car door.

* * * * *

Finn watched as two EMTs lifted the stretcher with Mr. Shore on it into the back of the ambulance. His daughter followed with Scott in her arms. He still breathed heavily from the strenuous exercise he'd had in the past hour as he and twenty other members of his crew had pushed and harried the medical vehicle through the rapidly mounting snow. He'd agreed on the phone with both the dispatcher and the ambulance driver to meet the vehicle at the closest open ramp at 55th street.

They'd followed the ambulance in several pickup trucks, stopping to push the ambulance through the snow whenever it got stuck. After a grueling journey Finn and his crew finally got the ambulance to a point that was within a quarter mile of Toni Angstrom's Oldsmobile—close enough for the EMTs to walk to retrieve Mr. Shore and also in a place that the driver could turn the vehicle around.

Finn turned when he felt a hand on his back.

"Jeez, your shirt is damp. And it's not from the snow, is it?"

He studied Esa's pale, drawn features through the snow that fell heavily between them. He'd been grateful as hell to hear her confident voice earlier, and not just because she was a doctor who undoubtedly could handle the distraught mother better than he could.

He'd been happy as hell because it'd been *her*. Period. He'd missed her like crazy over the past two weeks. And his desire to see her again hadn't faded like it should have if she was just some passing affair. It had grown until it became an annoying ache in his gut that wouldn't be quieted no matter what he did.

Despite his stupidity on Halloween, tonight the truth had struck him full force as he'd watched her handle the hysterical mother and wailing child like a pro. The idea of her being a physician seemed just as natural and right as the idea of her being a libertine publisher of a singles' magazine had always seemed somehow wrong.

He burned with curiosity. Why the hell had she lied to him?

"It's sweat," he answered Esa's question after a moment. "The ambulance got stuck five times."

She sighed shakily. "At least Mr. Shore is better off in that ambulance than in his daughter's car. Although I have to admit, he looked a heck of a lot better by the time the EMTs came for him. His color was improving and he was breathing more easily. Maybe it wasn't a bad heart attack. The aspirin seemed to help. I just hope the damage to his heart isn't extensive."

She bit her lip in obvious concern as she watched the EMT close the ambulance doors. "Scott's fever went down a little bit with the acetaminophen, as well," she added. He was taking liquid and resting quietly by the time the EMTs came.

"They were lucky to have a doctor there."

Flirting in Traffic

Her eyes leapt up to his face. The moment stretched taut as they stared at each other.

"*Why?*" he whispered hoarsely. "Why the hell did you lie to me?"

She shook her head and glanced away. "You thought I was someone else from the beginning. You saw what you wanted. You *wanted* me to be some kind of frivolous, casual fling. So I—"

"Gave me what you thought I wanted, like a good little actress?"

Her chin went up defensively. Her brandy-colored eyes flashed fire behind her glasses. "I gave you what you *did* want. Don't tell me you're going to deny it now."

"I don't deny that I wanted you but I would have appreciated not being lied to."

As soon as the heated words left his mouth, however, Finn wondered. Was he being as dishonest as Esa had been? Could he truthfully say that he'd been interested in anything more than a night of hot sex with a gorgeous woman that night at One Life? Would it really have mattered if she was the publisher of a singles' magazine, a waitress, a lawyer or a doctor? He immediately knew the answer to that.

Hell *no*. He'd wanted *Esa*. He'd wanted her naked, warm and willing in his bed. Maybe it'd been easier to propose sex on the spot believing she was a player but it didn't change the fact that he would have been wild to have her even if she were studying to become a nun.

He frowned when someone called out his name.

"I have to go. The ambulance needs an escort back to the ramp," he said.

Her face fell. "Oh, of course."

He dug in his jeans pocket and extracted his keys. He grabbed her chilled hand and wrapped it around them.

"The snow is letting up some. With some luck I'll be back in a little over an hour. These are the keys to the trailer. There's a bathroom there and a portable heater next to the desk. You'll be more comfortable there than in your car. Will you wait for me until I get back?" he asked intently.

Something hitched in his chest cavity when he saw the uncertainty on Esa's pretty face. "I made a mistake, Esa. Don't run again. There's nowhere to go this time."

She laughed softly when she glanced back and saw what looked like a massive parking lot instead of an interstate.

"Okay, I'll wait. I promise."

Relief coursed through him. He put his hand on her back. "Come on, then. The trailer is about a quarter mile up the road. I'll drop you off in the truck on the way."

Chapter Nineteen

Esa stood quickly when the door to the trailer opened an hour and a half later and Finn clambered up the steps, snow flurrying around him as he entered. The wind howled outside, catching the trailer door and flinging it wide. He shut it forcefully behind him and locked it into place before he staggered into the cluttered room. She not only saw him shivering but actually felt the cold coming off his body when he came closer.

"God, you're freezing," she said as she inspected his rigid features. She saw through the dim light provided by the gas heater that crystals of ice had frozen on his eyebrows and the dark gold whiskers on his angular jaw. He leaned over and held his hands to the heat appreciatively.

"The ambulance only got stuck twice. Didn't have as much of an opportunity to work up a sweat this time. We saw some Red Cross volunteers setting up shop along the way. You can get a free cup of coffee if you walk down a half mile."

Esa laughed ruefully. "Great. Just what people need."

He cast an amused glance her way. "Better than nothing, I guess. We're in it for the long haul. The Chicago Transit Authority officials are stopping people from trying to get on the 'L'. I'm betting that IDOT or the Illinois State Police are behind it. Getting the roads cleared is going to be impossible if everyone abandons their vehicle."

Esa shook her head incredulously. "New definition of a traffic nightmare."

"It's not all bad."

Esa met his gaze. "What do you mean?"

"At least the storm made it possible for me to see you again."

Esa looked away, unsure how to interpret his expression and tone. Wasn't he still angry at her for lying to him? And if so, wasn't it starkly at odds with the heat in his blue eyes?

"It wasn't so bad waiting. I found a copy of *Metro Sexy* on the desk and read it cover to cover. You know what?" she asked, striving for a light tone in her increasing anxiety about being alone with Finn. "I've been maligning my little sister. It's really a good magazine. Another thing I realized while you were gone. I understand now why your condo is so neat. Apparently this trailer is the place where you can express your slovenliness at full volume."

Finn straightened and glanced around the dim nine-by-fifteen-foot room. Over half of the floor space was covered by tables stacked high with files, tubes of blueprints and paper.

"This trailer has been like this for as long as I can remember. I didn't have the heart to change it after Dad died."

She looked up into his shadowed, handsome face. The ice crystals in his whiskers had started to melt in the warmth generated by the portable heater. It suddenly struck her how small the space seemed with Finn it, how dim the lighting was, how intimate it seemed.

She cleared her throat uncomfortably.

"I'm glad I ran into you tonight," she said.

His eyebrows went up. "You are?"

She nodded. "I never really got to tell you why I misrepresented myself to you. Do you want me to try and explain more fully?"

He examined her before he nodded slowly. "Yeah. Yeah I do. But hold on just a second…"

He went around to the front of the ancient, sturdy wooden desk and opened one of the drawers. He pulled a bottle of liquor out and hooked his finger in the handle of an empty coffee cup on his desk. The wheels of the chair that he rolled into position next to Esa clacked loudly on the tile flooring. He poured two fingers of the amber liquid from the bottle into the glass and handed it to her.

"What's this for? Courage?" she asked, her lips curving in amusement even as nervousness made her voice tremble slightly.

"If that's what you need it for," he said softly. "Personally, I need it to thaw out."

Esa smiled at him and was heartened to see that he returned it. The whiskey scored her throat as it went down but it didn't warm her anywhere near the way Finn's steady gaze did.

The words started to pour out of her mouth as though they'd been crowding eagerly on the back of her tongue for weeks now—which they had, she supposed. He never spoke, only listened with focused attention and took a sip of whiskey now and again.

"Finn, I want you to know that I absolutely forbade my sister Rachel to print anything in *Metro Sexy* about Julia and you," Esa said passionately once she'd reached the end of her story. "I don't know how Julia got her information but she was mistaken. Rachel would never have run that story in her column once I specifically asked her not to. Rachel may have her faults but she and I are very loyal to one another."

Finn stared thoughtfully at the flickering blue flames at the bottom of the gas heater. After a moment he roused himself, running his long fingers through his wind-tousled hair.

"I know it," he said.

Esa's eyebrows went up in surprise at the matter-of-factness of his statement. He gave a small smile and shrugged.

"I overheard part of your conversation with her on Halloween in my mom's kitchen. I'd been calling Rachel all week long, hadn't I?"

Esa nodded.

"I didn't get it at the time I heard the two of you talking but now that I know the truth it all makes sense. You were scolding her into not running the story." His small smile faded as she continued so study her in the fire-lit room.

"What I don't get is why you felt compelled to continue to lie to me about your identity after my initial error in calling you 'Kitten'."

Heat rushed into her cheeks. She looked into the fire to avoid his piercing stare. "It was stupid, I know… An impulsive, spur-of-the moment decision. Carla and Kitten—*Rachel*, I mean—had been getting on me recently for being so boring and lame. I'd started to realize they might have a point. I specialize in the care of older adults. I really enjoy spending time with my patients but lately I'd begun to realize that I'd been hanging around them so much in my free time because they were…I don't know. Safe? Nonthreatening companions for someone who had been burned in the romance department a few times too many and was going into early retirement?"

"And the night at One Life? What made you decide to take a walk on the wild side?" Finn asked gruffly.

"You did. I-I wanted you so much that I was willing to do anything, including pretending to be something that I thought you wanted—just so that I could be with you."

She'd spoken so softly that for a moment, when he didn't move or speak, she'd thought he hadn't heard her. The thought of having to repeat such an intimate confession made her panic momentarily.

But then she glanced up cautiously into his gleaming eyes and she knew.

He'd heard her.

He set the cup down on the desk and turned back to her. "Come here," he said, his voice rough and gentle at once as he reached for her hands. Esa's mouth still hung open in pleasant surprise by the time he pulled her into his lap and burrowed his long fingers through her hair. The whiskey and the gas heater had chased the chill out of him. He felt hard and warm beneath her bottom and thighs.

She moaned softly when he tightened his hold in her hair, bringing her mouth to his. He kissed her hard and masterfully, as though he wanted to stamp her with himself, stake some kind of primitive claim on her. Once she'd melted into him however, he softened his manner, lightly caressing her jaw and neck while his tongue plundered her mouth and his lips shaped and sipped at her own in a sinuous, erotic caress.

Esa's body seemed to erupt with heat as she luxuriated in Finn's taste, scent and touch. She'd missed him so much. It had been a constant pain that grew more and more sensitive over the last two weeks, every time the thought struck her that she'd likely never see him again.

A powerful need swamped her. She was distantly aware that not only did she claw at the buttons of his insulated shirt, his hands had also lowered and were hastily unfastening her blouse.

They broke apart a few seconds later and swiftly pulled the sleeves off each other's arms.

"I want you so much," Esa mumbled unevenly.

"I told myself it was best to forget you," Finn whispered next to her lips. "You were supposed to be a rebound fling. I tried like crazy to stop thinking about you but I couldn't. *God*, I've never known a woman who smelled half as good as you."

Her head fell back, giving his talented mouth full access. She shivered in excitement when he traced her spine with his warm fingertips and opened his hand over her waist. "Or who felt half so soft," he added between hot kisses on the front of her throat and chest.

Esa made a strangled sound when he lowered his face and nuzzled her satin-covered breasts from the valley between them with his nose and lips.

"You're so beautiful," he praised before he peeled back the cup of her bra from one breast and pressed light kisses on the curving flesh. He slipped a stiffened nipple into his warm mouth at the same moment that he shaped her other breast to his palm. Esa whimpered in pleasure while he drew on her so sweetly, making the throb between her legs escalate to a stabbing ache of stark need.

"Oh God, Finn," Esa groaned a moment later. Her hips shifted restlessly in his lap. His cock excited her almost unbearably as it pressed against her bottom, feeling large and deliciously erect. "Stop torturing me, please."

His head came up slowly from where he'd been inflicting said torture on her helpless breast. Esa bit her lip to stifle a moan when she saw how erect he'd drawn the taut, glistening crest. She squirmed in his lap but he stilled her with a hand on her hip.

"I wasn't torturing you, honey. I was in the process of making love to you."

"I know," she said shakily. Heat burned in her cheeks. "But Finn— *Oh!*"

Esa was temporarily left speechless at the sensation of him sliding his hand beneath her skirt and poking two long fingers beneath the elastic of her panties.

"How's that? Does that help matters?" he asked. He watched her through narrowed eyelids as he glided and pressed against her most sensitive flesh. Esa just stared up at him in mute desire as his fingers moved so deftly between her thighs. "It does help, from the look of things. And the feel of them," he added huskily. His nostrils flared in arousal. "You're very wet, Esa. Are you that wet for me?"

A groan of sheer desire broke free from her throat. "Yes. You know I am. I told you how much I want you."

"Enough to lie? Enough to pretend to be a wanton woman in order to have your sexual wishes fulfilled?"

"Oooh, *yes!*" she admitted. Her hips shifted up in hungry little gyrations against the erotic press of his fingers.

Finn smiled as he watched her, his expression tinged with wonder. "Maybe it wasn't a lie. You really are the most exciting, uninhibited woman I've ever met. You're like a package of dynamite. All I have to do is touch you and you're sizzling."

Esa grabbed at his shoulders desperately. Her eyes went wide. "Only for *your* touch, Finn," she whispered. She clenched her eyelids shut and cried out sharply as she exploded.

"Are you okay to stand?" she heard Finn say a moment later. Her eyes blinked open when she registered how rough with desire his voice sounded. She nodded and stood up. He came up behind her, pressing his belly to her back. She bent over the desk and put her hands on it when he exerted a gentle pressure. A soft moan of awakened desire vibrated her throat when she felt his hands slide her panties down to her thighs.

"Spread your thighs," he ordered tautly.

Esa stared sightlessly at the paper-strewn desk a moment later as Finn slid his cock into her. The sensation was so overwhelming, so powerful, that she began to tremble in uncontrollable excitement and raw need.

He must have sensed it because he paused and rubbed her hips, bottom and back soothingly. "Try to relax," he whispered hoarsely.

But the last thing on Esa's mind was relaxing as he resumed moving in her, his strokes long, sensual and slow. Much to her amazement she became aware that tears wetted her cheeks. He sank his flesh fully into hers and groaned.

The burn in her sex bordered on the untenable.

"God, you feel good," he said in a half-crazed tone. He leaned over her. "Give me your mouth, honey."

Esa twisted her neck and met him. Their tongues tangled erotically. His cock throbbed inside her, the sensation making her whimper into Finn's mouth. He nipped at her lips with his front teeth.

"I'm glad you're not a promiscuous sex kitten, Esa. It nearly drove me right over the edge to think of another man touching you."

"There is no other man," she whispered back. His eyes gleamed at her from the near darkness. He flexed his hips, stroking her with short, sensual thrusts.

"I like the sound of that."

"I do too," she said softly. "Oh Finn...I *know* I like the *feel* of that."

He chuckled and then groaned, the noises barely audible between the increasingly frequent sound of flesh slapping against flesh. Esa pressed back with her hands and moved her hips in synchrony with Finn's, craving the delicious friction that built and built and built until she thought she'd go mad from the intense pleasure.

"I can't take any more," Finn muttered wildly. His fingers found her clitoris. He rubbed as he crashed into her and growled like a feral animal.

"Oh...oh...oh, *yes*," Esa cried out as she climaxed, bucking her hips wildly along the length of his cock.

Finn slapped her bottom in gentle reprimand with his palm before he stilled her frantic movements with both hands. He held her still, buried himself deep and roared as he came.

When their ragged, wild attempts to catch their breath had quieted to mere heavy pants Finn withdrew, sat down and pulled her into his lap. He nuzzled her neck while Esa stroked his soft hair and a feeling of sublime contentment and warmth weighted her limbs.

"I'm sorry for putting a halt to things that night on the phone," Finn said quietly after a moment. "I was pretty...turned inside out because of the way I was feeling about you. I had myself half-convinced that it was just an infatuation following the breakup with Julia—sort of an emotional backlash. I wasn't very trusting of my judgment when it came to women. I saw a really ugly side of Julia that night she stopped by my condo. It really increased my doubts about becoming involved with someone else so soon after the breakup. The fact that you'd lied just made things more convenient, easier for me to put the brakes on the whole thing."

Esa leaned back and examined him when he trailed off. "Instead of facing the music about what was going on between us?"

He gave a slight grimace of acknowledgement.

"I understand," Esa said. She nodded when his gaze flickered up to meet hers. "I'm the one who's sorry, Finn. For so many things."

When she saw his eyebrows rise expectantly she tried to explain.

"I was trying to convince myself of the unlikelihood of the possibility of anything significant happening between us as well. Not just because I'd lied to you either," she said with a roll of her eyes. "I just didn't think it was very likely that I felt this way about a guy I'd only known for a little over a week."

He rubbed her hip. "We've got plenty of time ahead of us to quiet our concerns. We'll go at a pace that's comfortable for both of us, okay?"

"Okay," Esa agreed shakily before she hugged him. She buried her face in his chest, feeling happier than she'd ever recalled being…and a bit silly besides, because tears filled her eyes just like they had when Finn had first entered her body earlier.

She went completely still as a thought struck her. She lifted her head.

"Finn, the rest of your crew, where did they go after you guys saw the ambulance to the ramp?"

"Most of them, including Jess, decided to try to get home taking the 'L'. The CTA officials were letting them if they could prove that they were road construction workers and not abandoning their cars on the interstate. A few of them can't get home using the 'L' though. They're waiting in a truck outside."

He saw her panicked expression.

"*What?* We were so *loud*," she whispered in rising mortification. "They probably heard us making love. I didn't even think to quiet myself while we were—"

She blushed hotly as she glanced over at the desk.

Finn laughed and tilted her chin until she buried her face in his chest again. "No reason to hide the truth from the rest of the world, honey. You are what you are. A wanton, uninhibited...damn sexy woman."

She pressed her lips to his fragrant skin. "Only for you," she whispered.

"I wouldn't have it any other way," Finn said, his deep voice rumbling from his chest straight to Esa's widening smile.

Epilogue
Eight Months Later

&

"Uh. Uh. *Uh*," Glory Madigan muttered appreciatively as she circled her soon-to-be granddaughter-in-law. Molly Madigan raised herself from off her knees and flared the hem of Esa's ivory wedding dress over her shoes.

"She looks fantastic, doesn't she?" Molly asked, her eyes running over every detail of the simple, elegant but nevertheless magnificent gown that she'd designed and created for Esa's marriage to her son that weekend.

"She'll be the sexiest bride I've ever seen," Glory stated baldly. "It's going to be the shortest wedding reception in history tomorrow night. Finn won't be able to wait to get her into bed once he sees her in that dress, Molly."

Esa grinned happily and ran her hands over the soft material at her hips. "You really think so, Glory?" she asked hopefully.

"I *know* so. Finn has his grandfather's genes. Goes in for all the curves," Glory said confidently as she swept her hand down her own glorious, statuesque figure. "Sean was half-wild to get me into bed on the night of our wedding. He offended my mother by making off with me to our hotel room after all the toasts were finished. She was furious that we didn't cut the expensive cake she'd had made."

"The cake I made wasn't all that expensive but I do hope you and Finn will have some before Finn 'makes off with you'." Molly chuckled as she checked the seam at Esa's waist. "Everything is perfect with the dress, Esa. Rachel is picking up the shoes this evening, isn't she?"

"Yes, she'll bring them to the rehearsal dinner toni—"

"*Esa!*" someone bellowed from Molly's living room.

"Finn?" Esa shouted.

"Don't you dare come in here, young man!" Glory shouted fiercely. "Esa is in her wedding dress."

"Well, tell her to get out of it and come out here, quick. I've got a surprise," Finn called, this time from the other side of Glory's bedroom door.

Both Madigan women gave Esa a speculative look. Esa shrugged.

"At least it sounds like a *good* surprise. For a second I thought he was going to say that the deal for the new house fell through," she said, referring to the bright, sunny townhouse they'd just purchased in Lincoln Park.

She snuck up behind Finn silently a few minutes later. He stared out the picture window in his mom's living room. Esa's gaze ran over him hungrily. The monumental lust for him that she'd felt from the very beginning had only grown exponentially over the past eight months. Her love for him magnified it until sometimes she was sure she couldn't wait for her work day to be over so that she could attack him.

He wore a pair of casual cargo shorts that showed off his muscular calves, lean hips and tight butt. Esa reached out and palmed one of those delicious buns presently.

"Is this my surprise? If it is, I love it," she teased as she squeezed the taut flesh.

He spun around.

"Hey…you just deprived me of my surprise!" she pouted.

His blue eyes gleamed with amusement. "You can have all you want of *that* here in a second. In fact, I'm counting on it," Finn said before he kissed her all-too-briefly on the lips and grabbed her hand.

"Finn, we don't have time to fool around," Esa whispered as he pulled her toward the front door. "The rehearsal dinner is in less than two hours."

"Plenty of time," he assured her.

"But—" Esa stopped talking abruptly when a flash of red caught the corner of her eye. Her eyes went wide in admiration when she saw the shining red Dodge Viper sports car parked in the driveway.

"How do you like it?" Finn asked warmly.

"I *love* it."

"Good. It's your wedding present. From me."

Esa gaped up at him. Tears swelled into her eyes. "You bought that car for me? *Why?*"

"Because I know how much you love to drive," he said simply. He laughed softly when a tear skipped down her cheek. He stepped closer and wiped it off with gentle fingertips. "I think that's when I first fell in love with you, when I saw your face lit by the dawn as you sped down Lake Shore Drive."

"Finn—" She shook her head, too overwhelmed to speak for a moment. "I love you so much. Thank you. It's the sweetest gift I've ever gotten," Esa finally said brokenly.

"It wasn't an entirely unselfish gift." His eyebrows arched suggestively when she glanced up at him. "The completely finished new Dan Ryan expressway officially opens tomorrow. But for my bride-to-be...well, let's just say it's opened a little early."

Esa just stared at him for a moment as love seemed to fill and vibrate in every cell in her body. She recalled how his gift of a wide open piece of road had struck her so poignantly almost nine months ago.

How could he have seen that passionate, vibrant side of her character so clearly when Esa had been so bent on denying it?

Her voice trembled with anticipation and excitement when she spoke. "Let's go then, lover. I'm going to give you the ride of a lifetime."

A small smile tugged at his shapely lips. "That's what I was counting on, Esa."

The End

Also by Beth Kery

eBooks:
Come To Me Freely
Exorcising Sean's Ghost
Fire Angel
Fleet Blade
Flirting in Traffic
Groom's Gift
Subtle Lovers: Subtle Voyage
Subtle Lovers 1: Subtle Magic
Subtle Lovers 2: Subtle Touch
Subtle Lovers 3: Subtle Release
Subtle Lovers 4: Subtle Destiny
Through Her Eyes

Print Books:
Come To Me Freely
Exorcising Sean's Ghost
Fleet Blade
Naughty Nuptials *(anthology)*
Subtle Lovers 1: Subtle Magic
Subtle Lovers 2: Subtle Touch
Subtle Lovers 3: Subtle Release
Subtle Lovers 4: Subtle Destiny
Through Her Eyes

About Beth Kery

Beth Kery grew up in a huge house built in the nineteenth century, where she cultivated her love of mystery and the paranormal. When she wasn't hunting for secret passageways and ghosts with her friends, she was gobbling up fantasy novels and any other books she could get her hands on. As an adult she learned about the vast mysteries of romance and sex and started to investigate that phenomenon thoroughly, as well. Her writing today reflects her passion for all of the above.

The author welcomes comments from readers. You can find her website and email address on her author bio page at www.ellorascave.com.

Tell Us What You Think

We appreciate hearing reader opinions about our books. You can email us at Service@ellorascave.com (when contacting Customer Service, be sure to state the book title and author).

Why an electronic book?

We live in the Information Age—an exciting time in the history of human civilization, in which technology rules supreme and continues to progress in leaps and bounds every minute of every day. For a multitude of reasons, more and more avid literary fans are opting to purchase e-books instead of paper books. The question from those not yet initiated into the world of electronic reading is simply: *Why?*

1. *Price.* An electronic title at Ellora's Cave Publishing runs anywhere from 40% to 75% less than the cover price of the exact same title in paperback format. Why? Basic mathematics and cost. It is less expensive to publish an e-book (no paper and printing, no warehousing and shipping) than it is to publish a paperback, so the savings are passed along to the consumer.
2. *Space.* Running out of room in your house for your books? That is one worry you will never have with electronic books. For a low one-time cost, you can purchase a handheld device specifically designed for e-reading. Many e-readers have large, convenient screens for viewing. Better yet, hundreds of titles can be stored within your new library—on a single microchip. There are a variety of e-readers from different manufacturers. You can also read e-books on your PC or laptop computer. (Please note that Ellora's Cave does not endorse any specific brands.

You can check our website at www.ellorascave.com for information we make available to new consumers.)
3. *Mobility.* Because your new e-library consists of only a microchip within a small, easily transportable e-reader, your entire cache of books can be taken with you wherever you go.
4. *Personal Viewing Preferences.* Are the words you are currently reading too small? Too large? Too… ANNOYING? Paperback books cannot be modified according to personal preferences, but e-books can.
5. *Instant Gratification.* Is it the middle of the night and all the bookstores near you are closed? Are you tired of waiting days, sometimes weeks, for bookstores to ship the novels you bought? Ellora's Cave Publishing sells instantaneous downloads twenty-four hours a day, seven days a week, every day of the year. Our webstore is never closed. Our e-book delivery system is 100% automated, meaning your order is filled as soon as you pay for it.

Those are a few of the top reasons why electronic books are replacing paperbacks for many avid readers.

As always, Ellora's Cave welcomes your questions and comments. We invite you to email us at Service@ellorascave.com or write to us directly at Ellora's Cave Publishing Inc., 1056 Home Avenue, Akron, OH 44310-3502.

MAKE EACH DAY MORE *EXCITING* WITH OUR

Ellora's Cavemen Calendar

www.EllorasCave.com

Ellora's Cave Romanticon

Annual convention
for women who
refuse to behave

www.JasmineJade.com/Romanticon
For additional info contact: conventions@ellorascave.com

Discover for yourself why readers can't get enough of the multiple award-winning publisher Ellora's Cave. Be sure to visit EC on the web at www.ellorascave.com to find erotic reading experiences that will leave you breathless. You can also find our books at all the major e-tailers (Barnes & Noble, Amazon Kindle, Sony, Kobo, Google, Apple iBookstore, All Romance eBooks, and others).

www.ellorascave.com

Made in the USA
San Bernardino, CA
13 June 2015